More Than!

The Person Behind The Label

Edited by:

Gemma Van Praagh
John R Gordon
Rikki Beadle-Blair

Published June 2016 by Team Angelica Publishing,
an imprint of Angelica Entertainments Ltd

Design copyright © 2016 by Team Angelica; each contributor retains individual copyright in his/her contribution

The rights of the contributors to be identified as the authors of this work have been asserted in accordance with the Copyright, Designs and Patents Act 1988.

All rights reserved. No part of this book may be reproduced or transmitted in any form or by any means without written permission of the publisher.

Team Angelica Publishing
51 Coningham Road
London W12 8BS

www.teamangelica.com
A CIP catalogue record for this book is available from the British Library

ISBN 978-0-9569719-9-9

Printed and bound by Lightning Source

Foreword

More Than! is a project which was initially created to inspire children to engage in a piece of extended writing outside of the everyday requirements of their school work. We asked the students of Stoke Newington School to discuss, workshop and explore sexuality identity issues by asking them to look 'beyond the label' of LGBTQ people. What are labels? Why are we given them? What do they do? How can they harm or protect us?

It soon became apparent that this raised broader issues with some of our young people, such as: how it feels to be Muslim in the current political climate; why does a disability instantly dictate who people think you are? – and how it feels to be a 'geek'.

The response we had from our students was overwhelming, with over 800 children submitting poems, scripts, songs, interviews, articles and other forms of insightful, eloquent and inspiring pieces of writing.

Then, thanks to the kind efforts of many teachers, parents, governors and local members of our community the entries were read, marked and sorted into categories. We then selected approximately 70 students to take part in a development workshop-day lead by a fantastic team of artists, playwrights, journalists, actors, directors and writers. This day was remarkable to watch: students working alongside professionals to develop their work further, exploring form and potential final presentation of their piece.

This project has truly opened the eyes of all who have taken part, seeing the amazing courage, maturity and awareness that young people have about themselves and their surroundings as they looked 'beyond the label' to the heart of the people they discovered.

Gemma Van Praagh

Table of Contents

Hannah Finke 1
Hannah Ffychte 3
Minnie Court 5
Maliq Mussai-Mitchell 8
Eddie Smith 10
Joshua Clark 12
Hallelujah Tedja 15
Rinesa Neziri 17
Gunay Aksoy 19
Joe Halsey 21
Redrei Visaya 23
Elizabeth Fasulu 25
Joel Cooper 27
Skye Fitzgerald 33
Maya Isidore-Coyne 35
Basak Altundal Bektas 39
Jacob Fisher 41
Stella Mathias-Stanley 43
Orla Newnham 45
Lila Moar 47
Razana Djerkallis 49
Faezah Manga 54
Spike Sharkey 55
Baran Kayman 57
Gabriel Devlin 59

Name	Page
Ayse Atun	61
Fletcher Adams	63
Connie Lammiman	65
Deniz Aydin	67
Mia Truman	69
Kate Hyatt	72
Ceren Bektas	74
Louis Brine	76
Thomas O'Shea	78
Lily McKay	80
Ciar Wild	82
Lyra Robinson-Winning	85
Zoe Edwards	87
Servican Yeter	89
Lily Crooke	91
Leila Edelzstein	93
Louis Powell	95
Rione Nurse	97
Mack Quicke	99
Anisa Khatun	101
Flora Kessell	103
Sophia Rivera Ramirez	105
Berry Coleman	107
Edith Wright	109
Sam Simmons	113
Martha Jack	115
Marilyn Ferizaj	117

Lorna Beckett 120
Shay Snipe Gayle 122
Milly Mason 124
Cassius Burley..126
Rachel Finke 129
Tamar Singer 131
Daniel-James Straughan 134

Hannah Finke

There once was a lesbian, looked the same as you and me.
But if she begrudged then she would be judged and do agree,
That this is not right as perception needs an exception as do you and me,
And we all come down to the same old, plain old, you or me.

There once was a gay, looked no different to you or me.
But words were said and rumours spread and that poor, poor man he lost his head.
But please, do agree,
That this is not right, perception needs an exemption as do you and me.
And we all come down to the same old, plain old, you or me.

There once was a bisexual, looked the same as you and me.
She was misunderstood but inside she was good, and I don't have to stand here and make a plea,
Because, and do agree,
That this isn't right, perception is in dire need of exception as are you and me.
And we all come down to a plain old, same old, you or me.

There once was a man who felt drowned in his body
'I AM UNCOMFORTABLE' he'd decree.
Although uncomfortable he was in no way unlovable as many thought a transgender may be.
Please, please, I beg you to agree,
That this is not right as perception needs an exception as do you and me.
And we all come down to a plain old, same old, you or me.

And from this poem I hope you can see that we're all extraordinary,
We all have our quirks because that is the way the world works.

More Than!

Don't you dare say you struggle to see
We all come down to a plain old, same old, you or me.
But we still own ourselves in senses,
As you are you and I am me.

Hannah Ffychte

An Alternate World

Wednesday 28th August

Dear Diary

I didn't do much today. I went over to Joe's for a bit, but I had to go home at six because Dad was going to give me a cooking lesson. Dad says that when I'm older, if I ever get married, it'll be my job to do the cooking and the cleaning while my wife goes to work. It's not exactly what I had in mind for my future but, as Mum says, that's 'just the way it is'.

I don't see Mum much. She runs a massive oil company somewhere in America so she has to go to endless meetings, make phone-calls, organise all the financial stuff. We kind of rely on the women in the family to make the money, as does pretty much every single household on the planet.

Thursday 29th August

Dear Diary

Thursdays – and for us, more commonly known as 'Homework Thursdays'. Mum sits down with Johanna (my sister) and does biology and maths and everything else, while I huddle up in a corner with Dad and practise my needlework. Pretty old-fashioned I know, but Dad says it's necessary to know the basics of stitching because it means I will have something to do later on in life that will hopefully mean I won't die of boredom.

Friday 30th August

Dear Diary

Today Johanna came back from school and said that when she grows up she wants to be a mathematician. Mum was delighted

More Than!

– her mother had been a maths teacher. She started to talk to Johanna about famous mathematicians. They were all female. Mum never really talks about school and that stuff with me – I only remember the one time, when I asked Mum if I could be an architect. She said that boys can't be architects, that they 'aren't that good at spatial awareness, or maths and drawing, unlike girls.' Don't know how they figured that one out.

To be honest, I'm not that into maths, but I have always been fascinated by buildings ever since I was little. I have fantasised about designing my own mansion one day. It would be the biggest, tallest, most beautiful building in the world. It would have thousands of windows and so many rooms you couldn't count. It would have towers and turrets, endless corridors and tiny little places you wouldn't know were there.

Not many people know about my little secret, except Mum, but she doesn't really understand. Neither would Dad. Johanna wouldn't care. So sometimes I like to dream about another world where I would live in this house with my father, mother and sister. Where Johanna and I would go to school and where I would learn about maths and science and buildings. Where Dad would go to work, and so would Mum. An equal world. A better world. An alternate world.

Minnie Court

More than a Person, Behind a Label

Everyone is different and special
They should all deserve the same
But sometimes people are not equal with potential
Also that is their aim
We all need equality and diversity to help us and
We all need different types of people to show us
And lead the way
We are all born different and with a purpose and a meaning
We all need different people to give us what we need
To give us what we want
To give us life and freedom
To give us love and laughter
To give us fun and joy
To give us help
To make us understand that life would be boring if we were all the same
It is good to understand others and where they come from
In our community, there are lots of different people from different cultures
It is an education in life
Learning and Living
Side by side with others who are not the same
Imagine if now, people with a different race were not allowed to see each other
Or know each other
It would all be not right and strange
Imagine if they were still separated and could not see each other
That would just be wrong
We need people like this
Our lives would not be complete if we did not have each other
If we were all the same

More Than!

If we looked the same
Talked the same
Did everything the same
Because it has gotten a lot better and more fair and more equal over the years
We are all different
In our own ways
That's what makes us special and individual and independent
And we all need to be like this
We need equality
We need difference
We need a community which allows others who are not the same as us
Who understand and care for others who are not as privileged
We are happier together than apart
We are better together than apart
We are stronger together than apart
In England we have all sorts of people
We have Muslims
We have Jews
We have Christians
We have black people
We have white people
We have mixed-race people
We have gay people
We have lesbian people
We have bisexual people
We have transgender people
We have millions of people who are not the same
All different and individual and independent
And sometimes people are racist or sexist or homophobic
And it is all about who they are
And people use that as an opportunity to tease and bully
But they do not know that it is good to have these people
They don't know that we need these people
And that without them, our community is too the same
Not different and we don't want the same

More Than!

We want different
And that is what makes us what we are today
We have learnt from others who are not exactly the same as us
And used it to be good people
And that is exactly what we want to be

Maliq Mussai-Mitchell

An excerpt from a work of fiction, a first-person narrative by Shaun George, a 14-year-old black boy from Hackney, East London.

I had just finished a particularly difficult song in my piano lesson: I kept messing up *Clair De Lune*. I can't practice much at home because my parents don't know about my keyboard. I saved up all my pocket-money to buy it and hid it under my bed, but my headphones broke, so now I can only play when they're out. My dad wants me to only play sports.

Earlier today my piano teacher, Jesus Abdullah, asked me why I was feeling down. Soon it all spilled out: how I was bullied in primary school for being different, being called gay and other words meant to hurt my feelings.

Instantly Jesus started tearing up. I didn't expect someone like him to get emotional; he's such a big and strong guy. But then maybe, like me, he's only pretending...

'You see Shaun,' he said, 'when I was growing up in Africa, I also felt different. As I got older I realised I didn't particularly like girls, I liked the same gender as me. I thought there was nothing wrong with it, but the government didn't agree. I had to keep my relationship secret for years until he didn't want to hide anymore. We had a fight. I was scared he would get hurt. I should have protected him. I told him not to go, but he was determined.'

I had no idea being gay was such a problem in some countries.

'It ended badly. He tried to protest, took a bus into Lagos one night and painted "Gay Rights are Important!" all over the city walls. The people weren't angry at the vandalism, they were angry at his message, angry about who he was. He never made it home that night. The next day, the horror: big letters over the front page of the biggest newspaper in Nigeria, "GAY MAN STONED TO DEATH".'

Jesus broke down, tears soaking his cheeks. Then he carried on: 'I knew I had to flee the country. They had found a picture of me in his wallet and were searching for me. There was no point staying without him anyway.'

For ages I couldn't stop thinking about what Jesus told me that day, about being born in a country where homosexuality is illegal. This was ten years ago, he told me. Today, Jesus is married in a civil partnership and teaches the piano at my local secondary school. He says the sound of the piano washes the sad feelings away. Makes me think of how lucky we are. If the worst thing that happens to me is being called gay for wearing skinny jeans or being ridiculed for preferring the piano to football, that's okay... I'm glad that London does not have laws like that because there is nothing whatsoever wrong with being different in my opinion. Everyone should have the right to follow their heart, as long as it does not cause any harm to others – that's what I believe anyway.

Eddie Smith

The town hall in Brighton & Hove was grimly modern, with concrete slabs and glass on the outside. It wasn't a very glamorous building, and didn't look like the sort of place you would want to spend one of the most important days of your life in, but I suppose it did the job. Standing around in the autumn breeze, listening to the wind make its way through the trees and brush past the light, golden leaves, I had goosebumps all over my body, partly because it was cold and partly because of the building I was looking at. There were middle-aged men in waistcoats telling bad jokes and smoking cigarettes whilst I was thinking about what sort of person would have made this building and what for. My thoughts were interrupted when everyone started clapping as Kevin and Alex arrived to start their civil ceremony.

A civil partnership confers the same legal rights as a marriage but you can only have one if you are in a same sex relationship. However, you cannot have a civil ceremony in a church. Kevin and Alex had their civil ceremony in 2006 as it has only been legal to have same sex marriage in the UK since July 2013.

Everyone hurried in, their shuffling shoes echoing off the tall ceiling. A woman looking very important at the front of the room wearing a completely white suit and a very big hat hushed us, and a guitar began to play quietly, and Kevin and Alex walked down the aisle looking happier than ever.

The first ever known gay rights organisation was founded in Chicago, America, in the early 1900s. America also set up the world's first transgender organisation in San Francisco in 1966, which was also where the first Lesbian Rights Organisation in the USA was held.

The woman performed the ceremony in the most theatrical way

possible, which made everyone laugh, but she seemed to be happy and it looked like she was used to it. Once the ceremony was complete everyone clapped and cheered and threw flowers and confetti towards Kevin and Alex as they left the hall and made their way to the party venue. This was followed by the familiar sound of shuffling shoes on the wooden floor as everyone left the hall after them. Kevin and Alex jumped into a shiny black car that looked like a posh schoolboy's polished shoe, and everyone else got on a bus that was driven by a porky man wearing a bowtie and a tweed flat cap – which clearly wasn't his favourite outfit, judging by the look on his face.

When bus drivers were dressed like this in England, in the 1930s, it was considered to be a sin if you were gay, lesbian or bisexual and it was against the law, at one time punishable by death. It was not until 1979 that the Gay and Lesbian Humanist Association (GALHA) began campaigning in the UK, which led to gay and lesbian couples being able to have civil partnerships.

Everyone arrived at the party venue and began dancing and drinking and eating cake and spilling champagne down the front of their dresses. And there were Kevin and Alex, looking happier than ever.

'Like being a woman, like being a racial, religious, tribal or ethnic minority, being LGBT does not make you less human. And that's why gay rights are human rights, and human rights are gay rights.'
– Hilary Clinton

Joshua Clark

Tarred with the Same Brush

I am Me
My brain is a place where I can hide,
Where people can't touch, feel or see.
But that can't happen because of boundaries,
And judgemental people stereotyping me.
There are the boundaries that they set;
They tar us all with the same brush.

I wear a Hoodie.
People cross the street when I'm around,
They assume I mug the defenceless.
I want to be friendly with everyone,
I don't want people to look down.
Why can't people just hug the youth?
I am tarred with the same brush.

I am Blonde.
People don't see me as clever,
They think that I have more fun.
But I want people to take me seriously,
Not just flirt and laugh.
I intend to make my own way in life;
But I am tarred with the same brush.

I am a Child.
Adults push me aside to listen to others.
They say that 'children should be seen but not heard'.
I am not naïve or stupid,
I wish that adults would take me for real.
I'm not too young to understand;
But I am tarred with the same brush.

I am a male Ballet Dancer.
People laugh at boys who dance ballet,

More Than!

They think they are bisexual or gay.
I wish I could tell the world about it,
Not be scared to hear what they say.
Free to dance whenever I feel the need;
But I am tarred with the same brush.

I am a Girl.
My parents buy me pink clothes and dolls,
They force me to wear them.
But I want to wear blues and greens,
I don't want to play with button-eyed dolls.
I want to climb trees and ride bikes;
But am tarred with the same brush.

I am Gay
People tell me to 'man up' every day,
They insult me by calling me a poof.
Commenting on my sexuality
What does it have to do with them anyway?
Gay means happy so why can't I be happy?
I am tarred with the same brush.

I am a Chav.
Council-Housed and Vile,
That is what people think about me.
No class, no taste, no style.
So what if I preen myself every morning
And I like branded clothes;
I am tarred with the same brush.

I am a Muslim.
A woman on her way to work.
They think that I am hiding something
Behind my burqa and in my backpack.
I do not conceal weapons in my clothes,
I am not part of the Taliban or Al-Qaeda;
But I am tarred with the same brush.

I am a Person.
So do I have to be stereotyped?

More Than!

The judges enclose us in an imaginary box
They close the lid and shut it tight.
They do this to know what they are dealing with,
They're scared so they hide behind the label.
It doesn't matter what you wear, the colour of your skin or shade of hair.
It just matters if you are happy being you.

Hallelujah Tedja

Owning my Label

At this point my life has become so organised, so organised that it's messed up in a way. I've given up fighting, oh long time ago.
CREAK!
'Miss Warrings, I came by to remind you that your one p.m. appointment is starting in five,' she says, staring at her watch.
'Thanks, Shelly.'
I get up and grab my label as I shut off the lights and close the door behind me. I drag myself past Lyla, Hannah and Becca's room, sick of the same routine.
I let myself into Dr Pears' room. 'So, Naomi, what's on your mind?' he says, pretending to care.
'Sometimes I feel like my label is meant for me, but then I remember the word hasn't been used or said in a long time.' I guess I got into it today!
'Naomi, look, you can't do this, saying stuff like that, or you and I will get into trouble,' he says, looking all paranoid.
I lean in close and say, 'I got put in here and got given my label for going on a strike for equality and you're trying to prove that wrong! Don't even try it!'
There was an awkward silence until the buzzer went off and my hour was up.

It's been days of thinking and I made a risky decision. I've decided to escape and return the town to the way it was. I already had a plan. My one p.m. appointment was arriving, so this time I grabbed my label, snuck out some sleeping pills, shut off the light and closed the door behind me. I let myself in again and slipped some sleeping pills into Dr Pears' tea. He didn't suspect a thing. He walked over to his satchel and took out his new glasses, and by the time he had drunk his tea he was in a deep sleep in his armchair.
I disguised myself in his clothes and snuck out.

I'm breathing so hard and I make it to the woods with no sign

More Than!

of anyone chasing me. The world is turning so fast and...

'Aaahhh!'

A girl not much younger than me stands staring at me, dead on, and instantly I'm back on track.

'What's your name?' she says, tilting her head.

'Naomi.' I'm still restoring everything in my head.

'I'm Nancy, what's your label?'

'Trouble-maker. What's yours?'

'Low class,' she says, looking ashamed.

She looks at me with a concerned expression, as if she was trying to read me.

'There are some people you should meet.'

I'm intrigued so I follow her to this shed. She opens the worn-out doors and inside is a room of about thirteen people, all gazing at me. Then Nancy says, 'Guys, me new friend Naomi has something to say.'

I was on the spot so I just spoke what was on my mind.

'Hi. Well, I was held at TMH for fighting against labels and stereotypes, so I escaped to finish the job.'

'There's a meeting at the town hall next week,' says a boy who introduces himself as Rob.

And right then I knew what he meant. We spent the rest of the week planning and then the day arrived. We scattered and I felt as if it was all going in slow motion. The mayor stepped up to start speaking but was pulled back by Rob (his supposed bodyguard). I didn't think I'd get this nervous. The mic was right up to my lips and everyone was looking at me as if I was crazy.

'How can you restrict someone from going somewhere because of their label? The right question here is what a label is. Maybe you think a top doesn't match your jeans but you cannot do that to an actual person!'

And before I knew it, it went from a clap to a standing ovation. I turn to look at the mayor and he's long gone. I throw my hands up in victory because I've owned my label...

Rinesa Neziri

Some people judge and group others into stereotypes. Stereotypes play an important role in today's society. Stereotypical generalizations are generally negatively based on how different groups of people perceive others on their appearance, beliefs, behaviours or countless other categories that we put people in.

'DON'T JUDGE THE BOOK BY ITS FRONT COVER'

This is a great quote which the prejudiced should take into consideration instead of making instant decisions. By stereotyping, we hold back a person's characteristics, abilities, equality and individuality – which leads to categorization. Although most people stereotype, it is a wrong thing to do as the person is not who you think they are. It isn't nice and isn't always fair. There are different people being different but true, labels which are natural. Be yourself and stop trying to be someone else, no matter what people say and think you are or call you by.

EXAMPLES:

SKINNY = ANOREXIC
BLONDE = STUPID
WEARS BLACK = EMO/GOTH
YOUNG = NAÏVE
GLASSES = GEEK
PINK = GIRL
BLUE = BOY
MUSLIM = TERRORIST
INTO SPORTS (WOMEN) = LESBIAN
SUPER STYLISH (MEN) = GAY
ETC...

Most people feel too ashamed and embarrassed to show the world who they really are. This is caused by stereotyping, which has an enormous impact on how we feel. Stereotypes are everywhere and part of our everyday life. This, like the colour of your skin, your gender, age or anything, should not define who you are. A well-known celebrity, Beyoncé, said, 'Independence comes from you knowing who you are and you being happy with yourself'. As stereotyping involves taking a description of an individual and applying it to a group as a whole, stereotypes may ruin the reputation of a great community. As well as this, stereotypes may lead to people feeling isolated from a particular group, or may have a negative impact on some people, whereby these people are not what they are being stereotyped to be, but because they are being judged in such a way it may lead to them acting in that way and maybe even embracing the stereotype.

Many people think that they can tell if someone is LESBIAN, GAY, BISEXUAL OR TRANSGENDER (LGBT) by the way they look, dress or behave. This isn't always true. Here's a little poem for you:

WOMEN ARE WOMEN REGARDLESS OF SEX
AND MEN ARE MEN IN MOST RESPECTS
YOU CAN BE BOTH OR A MIX OF THE TWO
YOU CAN BE NEITHER IF THAT'S WHAT SUITS YOU
BUT PEOPLE ARE PEOPLE WHATEVER THEIR PARTS
BECAUSE WHAT REALLY MATTERS IS INSIDE OUR HEARTS

People around the world face violence and inequality and sometimes torture, even execution, because of who they love, how they look or who they are. This is really upsetting and depressing for some.

Gunay Aksoy

We are all the same. We are all going to die one day so there is no point in judging people for what they are and how they look. People might be gay, lesbian, bisexual or transgender – it is their own choice, it does not affect the rest of us.

When there is a group of girls in a sports team, people start talking behind their backs and saying they are all lesbian, or 'some are, but you never know'. A lesbian is a female homosexual, a female who experiences romantic love or sexual attraction to other females. That is how they want to live, it is their own choice, but what's upsetting is that they get left out, bullied, and people always think that they're different. Even if they are lesbians, what is wrong with that? It is a free world! You can be with whoever you want. Personally I think it is a waste of time.

Lesbians don't get treated as badly as gay men. They say all gay men are skinny and white. That is labelling people. We see so many white and skinny men, it does not mean they are all gay. In some countries groups of gangs kill gay people because of their beliefs. There is nothing wrong with being gay so I don't understand why people treat it as wrong: they should respect.

Judging a person does not define who they are. It defines who you are.

They say bisexual people are greedy, straight, confused but that is not true. Bisexuality is romantic attraction towards both males and females. It does not mean they're greedy just because they like two genders. This quote is really nice: 'You can close your eyes to things you don't want to see but you can't close your heart to things you do not want to feel.'

Transgender is the state of one's gender identity or gender expression not matching their assigned sex. They are not comfortable so they want to change their gender. It is not a choice. It is really hard for them, it takes a long time, and they take medication. I don't understand why they get left out. They are human as well. Not everyone is the same. I think this quote must make people think before they judge. It is by 89: 'It is not about becoming a new person. I am already who I am. I just want my body to reflect that; it is not like I'm suddenly changing from the person you have always known. This is more about your willingness to see who I have always been.'

Another quote, from Ellen DeGeneres: 'To me, beauty is about being comfortable in your own skin. It is about knowing and accepting who you are.' People should respect each other.

There is a story behind every person, a reason why they are the way they are. So think about that before you judge someone.

You only get one life. The choice is yours.

Joe Halsey

It was a big old oak tree that we all used to sit under. It was great fun to sit under the tree during the long summer evenings. We would lay on the grass and talk, and the boys chased their girlfriends around and the girlfriends would act all shy or flirt like mad.

Tim used to love those evenings, and no one could understand when he was no longer around why he had chosen to leave.

We now know Tim was gay. No one is really sure whether he had always known that he was that way, or how unhappy he must have been.

When we went to the church for his funeral, his dad said that when he came out to them he cried. His dad was never sure whether that was out of relief or fear. His dad said that he wished he had spoken to him more.

Tim had so many friends; we all thought he was so happy. There were times when Tim didn't come out and spend time with the rest of us, like the times when we would play football and go swimming. There were times when he wanted to be alone. But every time he was with us he was so funny. He was so popular and, most important, he was so happy!

Tim leaving was a shock. The way he chose to leave was really sad.

He was found on a Saturday night. It was the one Saturday night when the rest of us couldn't go to the old oak tree and spend time together.

Apparently Tim sat there for a long time on his own. He was found on Sunday morning hanging from the biggest branch on that old oak tree.

We used to love hanging around that oak tree. Now all we feel is sad, thinking about the incredibly unhappy life Tim must have had.

Was it because he didn't understand that he was gay? Was it because being gay made him feel as if nobody cared for him, and he was different from everybody else? Was it because if he was gay he felt that people would treat him differently? We will never know. All we will ever know is how much we miss Tim and how special he was.

The one thing we all talk about now is, why does society make people feel different? Whether you are gay, straight, have a disability, belong to a minority or belong to a religion that is different to most of the people that live and work near you, everyone should not only feel welcome and loved but we should value everyone. We all miss Tim but we are left with the lingering doubt that we could have loved a little bit more and cared for him a little bit better.

Redrei Visaya

Spoken word: Labels

Who has the right to give an absurd dictation?
　Who has the right to give a wrong evaluation?
　Who has the right to induce perturbation?
　Who has the right to label?
　Not you, not me, you your friends, not your girlfriend, not your boyfriend, not your sister, not your brother, not your mum, not your dad, not your auntie, not your uncle, not your cousin, not your grandma, not your grandpa, not your acquaintance, not your followers. NOBODY has the right or authority to give a label.

You walk down the street. You see a person. You have never met them before. Society gives them labels. They may be male, may be female, may be young, may be old, may be black, may be white, may be gay, may be straight, may be Christian, may be Muslim, may be Jewish, may be Sikh. They could be anything but you don't know that. Your brain gives them something. Something wrong. Something that you wouldn't say to their face. Something racist or sexist maybe. You give them a label.

This is what society does. It gives labels. Who said that all blonde people are dumb? Who said that all Asians have to be clever? Who said that girls are weaker than boys? Who said that boys are confined to the colour blue and girls to pink? Who said that white people don't have rhythm? Who said that all black people like fried chicken? These are wrong. These are labels.

Our leaders say that racism and sexism have been abolished. Look at our generation, what do you see? People on their phones, looking at their tiny screens, ignoring the fact that it's still continuing. All you have to do is join a simple conversation with anyone and you'll hear at least one racial joke or comment. The world's future generation, thinking that the world is free from racism and sexism, is wrong. This thing is the bane of society, this thing is a label.

More Than!

It's plastered on TV shows, on talk shows, on YouTube, on Vine, on Instagram, on Snapchat, on the radio, on our mouths, on conversations, on everyday life, on comedy, on cartoons, on plays, on our lives, on society and on humanity. It's everywhere. Racism and sexism is everywhere. We think that it's funny, it's satirical. It isn't. It's a label.

Walk down a street. Full of people. You can't go down one without being given a label. It seems like an automatic function. An automatic trigger to make you racist or sexist. It hurts that we do this to one another. You can't just look at someone and call them clever, call them dumb, call them a terrorist, call them an asylum seeker, call them an illegal immigrant, call them Christian, call them a Muslim, call them poor, call them rich, call them gay, call them straight, call them disabled when you never met them before. You give them a straight-up wrong label.

Who has the right to show an act of exploitation?

Who has the right to make a wrong revelation?

Who has the right to state that differences are an aberration?

Who has the right to be racist or sexist or even homophobic?

Who has the right to label?

Elizabeth Fasulu

Being gay reflects only on who you choose to fall asleep with at night.

It does not describe you as anything else.

Not your personality, looks, lifestyle, religion, views.

Anything.

Women are women regardless of their sex. And men are men in most respects.

You can be both or a mix of two.

You can be neither if that suits you.

But people are people whatever their parts.

Because what really matters is inside of our hearts.

Gay people should be able to get married. It doesn't matter if you think it's weird and unnatural, get over it! Nobody should be able to tell you who to marry because marriage is about love not gender. You should be able to marry someone if you love them, not because somebody else told you to. You shouldn't judge other people's lives because of who they like.

What if only gay people were allowed to get married? Straight people wouldn't like it, would they?

Gay or straight, everybody deserves to be able to live happily ever after.

What if a guy proposes to a girl? I mean, that's no different from a guy proposing to a guy!

I'm not lesbian or gay but I support their rights because I believe in the freedom of love.

LGBT people should not change who they are just because some people don't approve.

All we are is human. Nothing more and nothing less. Gay, lesbian, bisexual and transgender people are people too, you know.

Being gay is okay. Being lesbian is okay. Being bisexual is okay. Being transgender is okay. Do you know what's not okay? Judging people for something they can't control. So shut up and let them live their lives how they want to.

Not allowing gay marriage is not going to stop people from

More Than!

being gay... With that said, why not let people who are gay be happier in their lives?

I don't care if you're black, white, straight, bisexual, lesbian, gay, short, tall, fat, skinny, rich or poor. If you're nice to me, I'll be nice to you. Simple as that.

Gay people are human beings who deserve the same rights as everybody else.

Don't be afraid to show off your true colours. Don't be afraid to come out of the closet. There may be rude people who might judge you along the way but they're just going to have to learn to deal with it. Don't worry, you're not alone.

Life's too short to stress yourself with people who don't even deserve to be an issue in your life, because too much blood has flown from the wrists of people shamed for those they choose to kiss. I mean, so what if someone is gay? So what if someone is lesbian? And so WHAT if someone is bisexual or transgender? Why should you care? Why would you waste your time putting people down? It's completely normal to like someone of the same gender but I don't think people are really getting that. They don't understand the true meaning of love. Why exactly is falling in love so illegal?

So let's get this straight – if you don't like gay weddings blame the straight because they keep having gay babies. Marriage is a human right.

BEING GAY, LESBIAN, BISEXUAL OR TRANSGENDER IS OKAY!

THINK BEFORE YOU STEREOTYPE!

Joel Cooper

The stage is separated into seven small square bedrooms using lighting. Six of the bedrooms are in sections of an equilateral hexagon; the seventh is in the middle of the hexagon. ALEX, SARAH, BEN, ANDRE, LOUISE and KATIE are on computers in the six surrounding bedrooms. In the central bedroom is ANNABEL, also on a computer.

The words 'switch chat' are designed to be said robotically, to inform the audience of the location of the current messages.

The colour of the lighting will signify the location of the chat. Green equals a chat that everyone's in, red means the chat without Annabel, clear lighting means they are not in a chat. ALL except Annabel start in a red light; Annabel is in a natural coloured light.

Alex: hey all, my computer just crashed. What did I miss?

Sarah: not much, just deciding which is better, Oreos or Jaffa Cakes.

Louise: OREOS!!!

Ben: JAFFA CAKES!!!!

Katie: They're in completely different categories. Oreos is a biscuit, Jaffa Cakes are cakes. This is stupid!

Andre: That's what I've been saying for the last hour.

Ben: Jaffa Cakes are still better.

Katie: Just shut up idiot. Lol.

More Than!

Sarah: Omg guys, Annabel's on. What a loser! Since when did she get Facebook?

Alex: Lol, such a loser. Should we give her the initiation?

Ben: *(said quickly)* Yes, yes, yes, yes, yes, yes, yes, yes, yes!!!!!!!!

Katie: the chat's ready, let's go.

All but Annabel: switch chat.

All lights go green.

The new chat appears on Annabel's screen.

Annabel: Hey all, finally got Facebook. My parents are sooo stingy!

Katie: Explains a lot about you…

Annabel looks offended.

Katie: Lol kidding.

Annabel: Ohh, yeah, obvi.

Louise: Nobody says that anymore, sooo fifties.

Annabel: Actually nobody used language like that until the late nineties. In the fifties everyone spoke 'proper' English.

Louise: Sorry, smarty pants.

Katie/Louise: Switch chat.

More Than!

Katie and Louise's lights go red. Everyone else is still typing, but silently while not involved in the conversation.

Katie: Omg she is so moist.

Louise: She's probably a lesbian, have you seen how she dresses for school?

Katie: Ewww! It probably rubbed off from her dads. Once a Gaylord, always a Gaylord.

Louise: She's such a freak.

Katie: She stares at you in the shower rooms.

Louise: Ewww! She's such a pervert, just like the rest of her kind.

Andre: so Annabel, you're fifteen and only just got Facebook. How does it feel to be the latest person alive?

Annabel: It wasn't my fault, my dads just wouldn't let me and I asked them for years.

Andre: Didn't need to know your life story 'bored face'. Switch chat.

Andre's light goes red. Everyone else is still typing but silently while not involved in the conversation.

Katie: You escaped the freak then?

Andre: Ughhhh she's so boring. I don't understand how people manage to hang out with her.

Louise: Finally someone understands my pain. She thinks I'm her friend. Lol, no thanks!

More Than!

Ben: So Annabel, how's my top hoe doing?

Annabel: Wtf are u talking about?

Ben: I'm your pimp, you're my prostitute, it's all out. I mean look at how you dress, one day you're in the baggiest jeans known to man, the next a skimpy shirt and skirt for a three-year-old. I mean, make up your mind!

Annabel: You're such a creep!

Ben: Calm your tits! Switch chat.

Ben's light goes red. Everyone else is still typing but silently while not involved in the conversation.

Louise: You got bored too, then?

Ben: I'm telling you, she's a prostitute and a cheap one too, just too scared to admit it!

Katie: I knew it! Alex owes me a fiver.

Sarah: Sooo, I got a C in the geography exam, it was soooo hard. I mean population is just depressing, like, we are all going to die in the end!

Alex: Bit deep, Sarah!

Sarah: But it's true!

Annabel: I found the test easy. I mean it's obviously the Chinese government's fault for their population. They broke several human rights, including forced abortion and murder – it's messed up!

Sarah: I'm sorry smarty pants! Switch chat.

More Than!

Sarah's light goes red. Everyone else is still typing but silently while not involved in the conversation.

Katie: Then there were two!

Ben: He's such a flirt!

Louise: I think we need to tell him she's a lesbo!

Alex: Sorry about them, they're not the nicest people.

Annabel: I guessed.

Alex: So, I saw you around. Want to meet up sometime?

Annabel: I would love to.

Alex: How about this Saturday?

Annabel: Yeah, sure!

Louise: Switch chat.

Louise's light goes green. Everyone is still typing but silently while not involved in the conversation.

You do know she's a baby dyke?

Alex: Ewww gross.

Annabel: What are you talking about, I'm not a...

Alex: I've gotta go, sorry...

Alex's light turns off.

More Than!

Annabel: But...

Louise: Sorry, bitch. Switch chat.

Louise's light goes red. Annabel is still typing but silently while not involved in the conversation.

Ben: Hey, want to see something funny?

Katie: Go on then!

Ben starts rapidly typing.

Upload sound effect. A notification pops up in the top of Annabel's screen saying she's been tagged in a post.

Annabel: What's that?

She opens the notification. There's a message at the top, tiling it. The secret is revealed: twenty screen shots pop up of the open and private chats that have gone on.

Annabel: Oh...

She starts scrolling through the posts.

***ALL but Annabel**, in a random order, shout out all the names she was called in the chat.*

Fade to black.

Skye Fitzgerald

My name is Miko. I am a British citizen and have lived in England for most of my life. I have a degree in finance from a British university, but when people look at me or hear my voice, they don't see that. They see a foreigner. An immigrant.

My name is Emma. I am a lawyer and have a degree in law and one in science. I work at a very prestigious law firm and I've just been offered a promotion. But when I go out to celebrate in my high heels and short skirt, people don't see that. They see a slut. A sket.

My name is Jeff. I'm a charity worker and I love helping others, it being my job and also my passion as a person. I am a Christian and go to church every Sunday. But when people see me walking down the street with my boyfriend, people don't see that. They see a faggot. A weirdo.

My name is Katy. I can speak six different languages, and give talks on science in various universities and have a job as a lecturer. But when people see me stumble over my words when I write, because I'm dyslexic, they don't see that. They see an idiot. A stupid person.

My name is Ashley. I'm a teacher at a local primary school and love working with children and helping them learn. I've got a teaching degree and an English one as well. But when people see me going down the street in my wheelchair or a new parent comes to see me, they don't see that. They see someone with a disability. Someone different.

But we are all more than this. None of us reflect our labels or the judgement and stereotypes other people place upon us the first time they look at us. You're a Muslim, you must be a terrorist. But actually only about one percent of the terrorist attacks in the world are committed by Muslims. You're blond, you must be an idiot. But when has there ever been a study which proves this? You're a feminist, you must hate men. But feminism is more about the equality of the genders, not hating men. You wear short skirts, you must be a slut. But how does anyone know that? It might be quite warm outside, or it might just be fashionable at the time. How can we so readily judge people when everyone is unique?

Labels do not cater to everyone's differences. Sure, some blonds might not be that clever, but neither are some brunettes, redheads or any other person with any other hair colour. Maybe some Muslims are terrorists, but so are people from other faiths and cultures. You can't base an idea about a whole group based on rumours you've heard or facts about a minority. We are all more than our labels. We are all more than what you see on the outside. Let's stop pretending any different.

Maya Isidore-Coyne

'Anorexic Bitch'
A phrase thrown around without a second look.
A comment she takes with her everywhere.
From school
To the murky mirror above her mantle-piece.
A mirror blurred from her hot breath blowing against it as she tries
To find new flaws to cover.
Murky from the warm tears that attack the overwhelmed bags under
Her eyes,
Bags from the sleep she's lost trying to push the tears back down
So her mum doesn't hear her,
The pain building up inside her, and she swallows it down with one
Huge gulp,
A gulp that conceals the throbbing misery inside, from the world.
This beautiful young girl has been beaten by the constant comments
From people who don't even remember saying them.
People who don't notice the effects of their own words.
People who see her as just *the skinny girl.*
A girl who obviously doesn't eat, and thinks she's so sick, and obviously
She hates fat people, and loves being skinny, because well of course, she
Clearly chose to be skinny, there's nothing else to it, she's a skinny
Bitch.
Stereotypes.
You don't know her, or where she's from, or why she's skinny.
Why can't she be skinny?
Does your weight determine your characteristics?

More Than!

Who you are wasn't measured in stones the last time I checked?
Lanky f**k
Twig
Go eat some MacDonald's
Ew, what the hell, I can see your bones
Your legs are like chicken wings
I could snap you
Anorexic
Comments like this said without a care,
Without a second thought
Because they can't see behind the flat stomach, collarbones, and 'twig'
Legs
Your comment means more than you think.
She is more than just a skinny girl.
But her confidence has been crushed by all the words locked up in
That gulp of misery.
How dare you.
She is surrounded by negativity.
At school, boys laugh how 'flat' she is.
At home, she is constantly pinched with little comments from her
Younger sister, and older brother.
Her little sister who sings along to '*I'm all 'bout that bass, 'bout that*
bass, no treble' and '*I can shake it, shake it, like I'm supposed to do*'
As if women are meant to be a certain way.
Supposed to have a big bum, and a tiny waist,
Are supposed to '*shake it, shake it*'
And if you don't have a big bum and a curvy body, well you might as
Well listen to the lyrics her older brother hums along to.
'*F**k the skinny bitches, F**k the skinny bitches in the club*'
Oh Nicki, remember you before the bum and boob implants?
When your anaconda didn't?
When women were just women and not sexual images for the media

More Than!

to engulf.
When people saw people as just people!
Not labels.
The social effects of the media have made us have a certain view on
How things should be.
And how people should look.
When in reality, we are all the same.
We are all human, the same and equal.
'Real men like curves, bones are for dogs.'
So if you're skinny you are referred to as nothing more than a bag of
bones?
You're so misconstrued that you're only good enough for dogs?
The media devours any self-worth left for women who aren't 'curvy'
And allows it to spread throughout the world into reality.
Because the media is not reality.
And before Nicki entered the media, she was skinny too!
Tricked into the twisted view on how women should be today.
They should be able to live life, without being judged by whether or
Not they can put their whole hand around their wrist.

She was only a teenager.
Her body was still growing.
Her weight was never an issue until people started to comment on it.
That's when she got wrapped in all this madness circulating our
Society today.
As if *'you're so skinny'* is an acceptable comment but *'you're so fat'*
Isn't.
As if everybody chose the way his or her body looks.
As if this beautiful young girl wasn't *right*.
Making it down for dinner in a hurry, and shoving second helpings of

More Than!

Mash potato down her thin neck, with tears in her eyes as it hits her
Unprepared little stomach.
She runs up to her room to escape the concerned mum's lecture, and
To escape the world.
But she can't escape it when it's trapped inside her and she is gulping
It down.
She bawls into her pillow, until the bags under her eyes become sore,
The contents of her dinner is now inside a bin-bag on its way to the
Dump.
Her body isn't used to the amount of agony she's forcing upon herself.
No school uniform day tomorrow!
She nods and smiles through the pain.
Because that means she has to find something to cover up her body.
Nice baggy sleeves to hide the *disgusting pencil thin arms*, and maybe
A pair of 'lovely' flat pumps she hates to hide the fact she's a
Lanky
F**k
Why should she miss hours of sleep to hide tears from her own
Mother?
And fall asleep in class and get kept behind,
Pretending to be sick to avoid the pathetic labels people slap onto her
Name.
Just ignore them you might say,
How? When her mind constantly repeats the phrase
'Anorexic Bitch'

Basak Altundal Bektas

People are taking their own lives due to bullying from either peers or family due to being homosexual, bisexual or transgender. That is not acceptable in many people's eyes (including mine) because the decision to be either homosexual, bisexual or transgender is only that *specific* person's decision and they should not be judged on something as simple and ordinary as that.

In December 2014 I found out about Leelah Acorn, previously known as Joshua Alcorn. She's a seventeen year old girl who committed suicide due to the disappointment of her parents because she (he) wanted to be a girl. Leelah's story went viral when more and more people started to read her suicide letter on her Tumblr page.

She starts off her letter by saying, 'If you are reading this, it means I have committed suicide and obviously failed to delete this post from my queue.' She later on says how her life wasn't worth living because she was transgender. She says she had felt as if she was a girl in a boy's body since she was four, and when she found out about 'transgender' when she was fourteen she 'cried from happiness'.

When she told her parents about this, they reacted negatively. Her mother sent Joshua to therapy, but only to Christian therapists, (who were all very biased), so s/he was getting told the same things that his/her mother said and didn't get the therapy needed to cure his/her depression. S/he got told that s/he was wrong, selfish and should seek God for help.

She ends her letter by saying, 'Fix society. Please.'

A few days ago, while I was scrolling through one of my social media accounts, I came across a video. It was of a seventeen-year-old gay boy called Austin Wallis. His YouTube video, called *Be the Change: gay rights*, attracted a lot of attention and anger. Not anger towards him, but towards his old, homophobic head teacher.

When the head teacher of his old school found out he was gay he called Austin to his office. He told him to either delete all social media and hide the fact that he was gay or leave. The fact that he went to a private school made this legal.

Austin Wallis talks about how it is ridiculous that in this day and age you can be excluded from your own school for being gay. When he came out, he knew there were going to be people that were not okay with it, yet he never expected it to be from the people who were supposed to protect you from the bullies. He didn't give any names of staff or the name of the school because there were members of staff who had supported him and he didn't want the video to reflect badly on them.

What I find unacceptable in these two stories is that the discrimination came from people you would've least expected it to. I have heard that, in many instances, families have kicked their children out because of their sexuality. The only thing I have to say about this is that *if you really loved your children, friends etc, you would accept them for what they are.*

Jacob Fisher

A Stereotypical Story?

The young man walked into the club. Strobe lights lit up the dance-floor and made people's clothes flash different colours. He glanced back towards the entrance and the bouncer nodded to him as he made his way towards the bar and ordered a drink. As he leant against a wall and took a sip someone bumped into him, spilling his drink. The guy turned round and punched him in the face. He fell to the ground and heard the sound of his glass smashing. The guy landed another punch but then the young man felt the weight lift from his body. He looked up. There was the bouncer he had seen earlier, holding the man away from him with one hand. 'What a thug,' he thought. 'He must be so strong.' Then he blacked out.

Dave sat down on the soft sofa and took a sip from his mug of coffee. He didn't relax: he had somewhere to be tonight. He finished the coffee then put the empty mug down on the table, got up and took his coat off the hook, then went out the front door and locked it behind him. As he walked down the street people quickly moved out of his way. He made his way towards the warehouse at the end of the street. That was where he would meet them tonight.

The young man opened the locker marked Graham Richards, took out the possessions inside. Graham then left the building, turned round to look at the sign stating *Copperfield Hospital*, and strolled down the street until he reached a small blue car, which he got into, and then drove off. As he was driving he began thinking about last night and the idiot who had punched him. Also that bloody bouncer who hadn't even done anything about it. It's not that Graham wasn't grateful – he had pulled the guy off him – but that's all they were good for, muscle work. It's not like they did any thinking. Anyway, they should be

More Than!

keeping watch for people who look like trouble, but they're so slow, so even if they did see, it would take too long for them to get there. He continued driving.

Dave got ready. He had a big job tonight and he wasn't going to screw it up. He'd put a lot of effort into this. Tonight was his night, tonight was what he lived for. He put on his jacket and left his house: he should probably set off now if he wanted to make it in time for the show.

Graham got out of the car and put his hand in his pocket and brought it out again, revealing a ticket for the Royal Ballet. He passed it to the man in the box office, who punched it then waved him through. He went in, walked through to the theatre and took his seat. The curtain rose and the first dancer came on and began. It was the bouncer from the nightclub and it was beautiful.

Stella Mathias-Stanley

We're racist and that's the way we like it!

On Tuesday 17th of February, on a Paris metro train, a man known as S. Soulemane was racially abused by three Chelsea supporters who refused to let him on the train. This is his story.

1 hour before the incident.

I briskly walked down the brightly-lit corridor, hanging my stethoscope round my neck, feeling the cold plastic on my skin. I walked past patients, narrowly avoiding flustered paramedics pushing hospital beds, carrying patients you could barely see amongst splints and bandages.

I set down the final blue folder on the receptionist's desk, handing in the last paperwork of my long shift. Heading back to my office, I heard the faint blow of a whistle from a radio hidden snugly under the circular desk.

I pulled on my coat, slinging my rucksack over my shoulder. My mind recalled events as I proceeded out through the doors, feeling the cool night air nipping at my hands. I walked down the subway steps, the smell of ammonia stinging my nostrils, and the glowing red letters of A&E disappearing out of sight.

The rush hour was underway. People in long black coats wearing ties and blazers bustled past others wearing white-and-blue scarves, muttering over the sounds of screeching wheels.

I dodged my way through the crowds towards a tunnel that led to the train that screeched as the brakes were hit and slowly pulled into the station. Heaving the bag back over my shoulder I walked towards the nearest car, my eyes falling on the distinct scarves and blue shirts attached to a group of boisterous-looking men.

Eager to get home I passed through the dispersing crowd as everyone spread out, anxiously waiting as the metal doors parted. I, myself, prepared to step up past the gap but I was

More Than!

stopped. The three men who I had taken notice of earlier stared out at me as if I had just rudely insulted them. Thinking of them as just a bit drunk I proceeded again to lift my foot to enter the train.

What looked like the eldest of the three put his hand on my chest and pushed me off. They all began to say repeatedly, 'No, no, get back, you're not getting on this train!'

They had the tone of firmness in their voices but I could blatantly see the image of humour pasted on their faces. I objected and tried again. I stumbled, the feeling of confusion and anger welling inside me. This time all three grabbed me and forcefully shoved me back again. I stumbled, now knowing the worry I felt as well was not unnecessary.

I couldn't believe what was happening or the idea of what was causing this. Their looks of humour turned into disgust as they now began to laugh, shouting stereotypical racism in my face. The events that were unravelling before me were unreal. I used to think society had come past this, and that this level of racism would not reveal itself in a busy train station. I knew these men weren't going to let me on as they continued to hurl abuse at me, purely based on the colour of my skin.

The doors began to close, but they leaned out, continuing to chant, 'We're racist, we're racist and that's the way we like it!'

Slam! The doors shut completely, leaving me in the aftermath.

That chant rang in my ears, the looks of judgement imprinted in my mind. To think that people still feel the need to say that to whoever they like. To think that some still won't see me as a person, but as a black person. For me, it's a humiliation. I was humiliated in my country. I was humiliated in front of my family, humiliated in front of my mother and father, my children. How can I tell them that this is what they may have to deal with when they enter a world where this is still happening?

Orla Newnham

I leave the house and don't bother to lock the front door. Rain whispers across my face and the pavement moves softly beneath my feet as I walk. The city is beginning to curl up on itself as the winter night closes in. I walk away from the hum and buzz of the main road to where the carts limp painfully through the streets instead of thundering around corners like angry bullets.

I reach the eerie wasteland that is Butterfield Green at twilight and walk through the creaking gate. Grass crunches beneath my boots as I walk to the bench hunched at the top of the hill. I sit, the cold metal seeping through the seat of my jeans. A lone pigeon picks at a scab of food nearby. I watch it, wondering how easy the scavenging pest's life must be. No family to worry about, no pressure to wear the right clothes, no need to question your sexuality. An ignorant, meaningless existence, but a blissful one.

I tilt my head back to look at the sky, searching for a star to wish on, but of course London's pollution has hidden the wonders of the night from my eyes. Not only do I have to face bullies, an unaccepting family, a confused sexuality, but there isn't even a burning ball of gas millions of miles away to help me wish my problems away.

It's hard y'know? Being different. Personally, I don't even see what the big deal is. Just because I like guys and gals, does that really make me so different? So weird? Love is love, whether it's straight, gay, lesbian or whatever. So why do I feel so ashamed, so horrified of one of my own qualities that I can't change? Maybe because I know that everyone all the time is judging me on something I have no control over.

My sexuality doesn't define me. It never has, it never will. And yet some people seem to think it does. They think there's nothing behind my label, no character, no personality. But I have other labels, more meaningful ones.

Daughter, granddaughter, niece, goddaughter, sister, guitarist, reader, actress, tennis player. Surely my hobbies and family members define me more than which gender I like?

More Than!

People like to pretend that the world is changing. 'Look back on how we were before. See how far we've come. Surely we can keep getting better?'

But it's not getting better. Being straight will always be the norm, and anything other is going to stay weird and different and strange. My sexuality doesn't define me, and it shouldn't define anyone else. The impact I have on other people, on myself, the mark I leave on this world. Those are the things that make me who I am.

And despite what others think, despite the labels, the stereotypes, the apparent desire others possess to drag me down, depress me, change my personality...

I'm frickin' awesome!

An aeroplane passes overhead. I remember the wish, the words that were swirling around my head when I first sat down. PLEASE MAKE ME STRAIGHT. PLEASE MAKE ME NORMAL. But the wish I make now on the blinking, man-made star-substitute is different.

PLEASE LET PEOPLE SEE ME AS MORE THAN JUST BISEXUAL. PLEASE DON'T LET MY LABEL DEFINE ME.

The aeroplane drifts through the orange haze above and twinkles out of existence behind the trees of the green.

A slight smile on my face, I stand and walk home through the heavy darkness.

Lila Moar

It's nearly spring and the weather is hot
Everyone is happy, no-one is not.
I came in from outside to get my lunch,
Where I saw that boy who stood out from the bunch.

There's always that person sitting alone,
You know, the boy with the book and not one friend to call his own.
So one lunch I decided to go and say,
'Do you mind if I sit with you and talk, chat or play?'

He looked up from his book and gave me a smile,
A smile that made me feel like I could fly for miles!

'I don't mean to hurt you,' I said to the boy,
'But I can't help but wonder why you don't enjoy,
Being at school and having fun,'
But then his smile dropped and his face saddened a ton.

I instantly felt terribly bad,
For making this poor boy feel so sad.
He noticed my look and said to me,
'It's not your fault; I just used to be…'

He paused and thought for a while,
'I used to be bullied,' and he began to cry.
'Can you tell me why? You don't have to say.'
He mumbled the reply, 'Because I'm gay,'

I couldn't believe what he said to me,
It's just plain ludicrous, sad and silly.
To think someone got bullied as if they were dirt on a table,
The bullies didn't see behind his label.

They thought he was a softy, all wet and pink,
They didn't know, they didn't think.

More Than!

I told the boy about LGBT week,
He just gazed at me, looking all bleak.
I said that it helps kids and teens day by day,
Learn that it's fine to be lesbian, homosexual, transgender or gay.

He said, 'People just see the stereotypes of being gay,
They never see me for who I am or hear what I say.'
Stereotypes should be defied,
Whether you're thick or thin, tall or wide.

The boy now has confidence and he went to tell his dad,
From now on he is happy and never, never sad!
He's got some friends who are nice and kind,
No-one care that he's gay, no-one minds.

Labels are hard to escape once they've been placed,
Some have a bitter-sweet not-nice taste.
But if bullies are about, and they don't see you for who you are,
Then tell an adult or a teacher, it will make things better by far!

Razana Djerkallis

My Auntie Penn

Mum and Dad were going out *again*, to who knows where, on the first day of the Easter holidays. Which meant me and my two brothers were stuck with Auntie Penn with her annoying jangling bangles and even more annoying high-pitched giggle. I usually just try to stay out of her way. She acts all lovey-dovey, grabbing me to ruffle my hair and kissing me 'mwa!' on both cheeks, but I know it's all an act. She probably just wants to get it over with. There's something fake about her. I went up to my room and, putting on some Sam Smith, I grabbed my football and threw myself onto my bed. There was a knock on my bedroom door and Auntie Penn poked her head round. She frowned when she saw me and said, 'Aren't you ready yet, Sam? Your mum and dad are done be here in less than half an hour and they're expecting you ready when they get back. You know how worried Nan gets if you get there late.'

I waited until she had left and then threw my football into the air, once, twice, and then the third time I missed and it bounced against my wardrobe. The door swung open and I grimaced at the girly dresses and embroidered trousers my mum had bought me. Life must be so much easier for my brothers. I've been a tomboy ever since year 2 or 3 and it's always been fine. Now I'm in my first year at Secondary School, and suddenly my friends have turned boy-crazy and spend all their money on makeup, and I don't seem to fit in anymore. I knew I was expected to wear one of those hideous dresses to visit Nan, which clung to me in all the wrong places and made me itch. I was dreading it.

The first day back at Felix Secondary School was one of the worst days of my life. I was alone again in the school library trying to pass the time. Back in primary school I was popular, either playing footie with the boys or hanging out with the girls. I always had someone by my side and was looked up to. I suppose I didn't realise what I had until it was gone.

Eventually the bell rang and I made my way to drama class.

More Than!

Mrs Sinder, our drama teacher, told us that for our homework we had to write a 500 word story from the viewpoint of a Lesbian, Gay, Bisexual or Transgender adolescent as part of LGBT Month.

When we were packing up our stuff, Megan and her friends walked up to me with smirks on their faces. 'Hey Sam,' Megan sneered. 'How's it going? You know the LGBT homework? Well you're gonna find it mega-easy. You can just base it on yourself because, you know...'

'W-w-what?' I stammered.

'Oh come on Sam! Awwwwww! She doesn't even know herself! Oh, silly. You're a lesbian!'

Megan's friends started whispering, and then one of them asked Megan, 'Hey, do you think she likes me?'

Megan looked me up and down, sneering at my short hair and trousers. Another of her friends said, 'I hope she doesn't like me!' and they dissolved into giggles. By this time we had a bit of a crowd round us. Megan and her friends ran away from me, screaming and laughing. A few of the watching pupils laughed; others gave me pitiful glances, and most kept their heads down, pretending they hadn't heard a single thing.

After school I didn't feel up to going straight home so I walked up the hill to the local library. It wasn't the best of libraries; it wasn't very big and needed redecorating, but it had a small study space that I often used at the back, and that was good enough for me. I sat myself down and got out a blank piece of paper for my LGBT homework. I stared at the blank page seemingly getting larger and larger, until it seemed to swallow me up. I felt scared and I didn't even know why.

'Maybe Megan is right,' I thought to myself, 'and I *am* a lesbian... Or maybe Megan is wrong and I'm not. Or maybe I should stop letting Megan get to me.'

I quickly took out my maths homework. I read the same question again and again, not being able to take anything in. My eyes started to wander until I caught sight of a small table at the back of the room that was full of posters and leaflets. I picked up my stuff and wandered over there casually. I skimmed over the posters advertising baby yoga classes (whatever they are!), as well as judo, gymnastics and babysitting services. I then looked at the displayed leaflets on anti-

More Than!

cyberbullying, cancer, domestic violence, dyslexia... And that's when something caught my eye. I stuffed it into my rucksack and took the bus home even though it was only two stops. My legs had gone numb.

By the time I got home I was almost crying and I didn't even know why. I was so relieved to see my mum at home – even though she hadn't paid much attention to me these past few months – that I practically knocked her flying.

'For goodness' sake watch out, Samantha!' she said irritably. I started to tell her what had happened at school but Mum just pushed past me, muttering, 'Tell me later, Sam,' and locked herself in the bathroom without giving me a second glance.

I ran upstairs and, in a rush of rage, I grabbed my dresses, my hairclips, my pink teddy bear, my flowery photo-frame, and then anything at all remotely girly, and shoved it all into my wastepaper bin. It overflowed and I kicked it over. When I could catch my breath again I took out the crumpled piece of paper from my rucksack and started slowly smoothing out the creases, wishing I were smoothing out the creases of my life. Holding the leaflet carefully in one hand, I slipped into my computer chair and gingerly started tapping out,

www.askjanet.org.uk

Once on the website I read the introduction:

Here you'll find a whole range of issues. Sometimes you can sort out a problem on your own and sometimes you can't. If you have a worry you can't cope with on your own, don't bottle it up, confide in a family member, one of your friends, a carer or maybe a teacher. A problem shared is a problem halved. You can also contact Janet at any time for help and support.

At the bottom of the page there was a picture of a smiley lady with a speech bubble saying:

My name is Janet and you can message me on this website any time you like, if you have a problem or feel lost or confused. You don't have to feel that you're alone.

I clicked on her and, slowly at first, but gradually building up speed, I typed,

This is Sam.

I'm not sure who I am anymore. I feel sick and confused. Now I'm in year 7 I don't have any friends anymore, and

today I was laughed at and called a lesbian. I like my hair short and I wear shorts or trousers but I'm not a lesbian, I think. In my head I've recently begun to think I'm a boy and that makes sense for a while, but then I begin to feel even more lonely and confused. My family doesn't have time for me. I used to be close to my mum but now she doesn't even speak to me; I feel like a failure. I have no friends and now it feels like I have no family either.

Please help me Janet.

At the exact moment I was about to press send there was a knock on the door. It was Auntie Penn. She told me that Mum and Dad had gone out again, which meant she would be looking after us again. She then smiled and asked if I was all right. I suddenly burst into uncontrollable sobs, and in an instant she was by my side. That's when it flashed across my mind – 'confide in a family member' – and it all came pouring out.

It's less than an hour later and I feel like a completely different person. I'm helping Auntie Penn with the laundry and I can't remember feeling so happy for so long. It turns out that Auntie Penn is a lesbian! She told me that the hardest part is telling someone how you feel for the first time, so now things will get much easier for me. She also told me how my life's just started, and I don't have to figure everything out at once. So yeah, she then read the message I was about to send to Janet, and that's when Auntie Penn also told me that Mum loves me so much and just hasn't been feeling well lately.

One last thing Auntie Penn said that will always make me smile is that, no matter what, she will always be there for me, every step of the way. I started to cry again as she put her arms around me and promised she'll always love me and help me, and although it may seem bad now it will sort itself out in the end. Apparently, when she was a teenager, my mum helped her and was so supportive through a difficult time in her life. After the talk I realised that Auntie Penn was absolutely right. Why rush my life and panic when it's just started? Why worry or let other people say who I am and what I am when I know the answer. I'm Sam, Samantha Wells. I have two brothers, a mum and dad and one amazing auntie. I am also a Sam Smith fan

More Than!

and Man U supporter ;). I feel guilty for thinking Auntie Penn was fake or something; she's the most genuine, unique and wonderful person I have ever met and I hope I never, ever lose her.

While I was still helping my Auntie Penn with the laundry, the doorbell went. There were Mum and Dad on the doorstep, looking happy but exhausted. They walked though to the kitchen and Mum bent down and whispered into my ear, 'I'm so sorry we didn't get to speak earlier, I promise I'll make it up to you later. In the meantime I have some news that you might like to hear.' At that point Dad called my two brothers into the front room and the news was given: Mum is going to have a baby. We are also going to move in a few months. My fresh start. I went up to my room to carefully take my stuff out of the bin. Instead I packed it all into a cardboard box and, taking a pen, I wrote on the front:

"For My Little Sister"

Faezah Manga

Hi, my name's Ollie and I'm a boy, but to say the truth I don't want to be one. It's just I look like trash and HATE everything that boys should like. I play with dolls and have long dark hair and put it in a ponytail. But who cares about other people's opinion. Yeah, so what if I'm gay. So I have decided when I'm suitable enough for plastic surgery, I will be a transgender.

Yes, yet I'm not sure about my parents. What if they kick me out of my house? But I have FREEDOM OF SPEECH! I can be who I want. Luckily enough my mum's an actor and my dad is a builder so we're basically rich. I have a girly room unlike anyone's, and people never accept me for who I am. In school I get bullied and get called DRAMA QUEEN. It's just pathetic how people can label you so easily. This is why I have no friends.

BUT I'M JUST A PERSON AND I HAVE FEELINGS!

There's a thing in my town that's weird. They don't like homosexuals. There's a saying, 'Be one and get out or stay and live'. The most horrific part is that they skin you alive if you are. That's what happened to Leevee Dunkan. Long story... (I don't know how to make it short.)

Also it's annoying how I can get judged easily. I will say it out loud! I AM GAY AND PROUD! I don't care about people's opinions.

Later on, when I grow older, I want to help people be confident, and be helpful to people who are let down by others. I am happy to turn into a girl. People can label me however they want. The town rule will go down and we can all be who we want. Also, I can ask my parents. It's risky but it doesn't matter – I'm gay and proud.

Spike Sharkey

In 77 countries around the world
Same-sex relationships are a crime,
And 5 of those, we are told,
Use the death penalty, so it's time

It's time to change
The way we think
It's time to change
The way we speak

You might not think it's that bad in Europe or the USA
But in these countries abuse is reported every single day!
Hold on a second, let me just say,
Why do people think there's a problem with being gay?
It's completely insane, I don't understand
These people who buy their heads in the sand.
Prejudice is a problem,
And when you ask why,
These people just give a shrug and a sigh

The only thing that makes gay people different
Is their sexual orientation and that isn't
A legitimate reason to steal their human rights
'Cause this kind of thing leads to apartheid and fights!

Some kids these days are raised to think that gay is an insult,
'That's so gay' 'You're so gay' and this carries on as an adult,
It's not a life-choice, or a frame of mind,
We now need a youth petition signed!

But even with all this doubt considered,
Hate crime across the world has certainly triggered
A worldwide revolution of LGBT rights,
And a peaceful solution is still in sight!
Take Russia, for instance, a cage of homophobic hate,
Where brave gay people and activists stand up for the sake

More Than!

Of human rights and equal love, all on the side
Of freedom of expression and community pride

37 American states passed the law
That gay marriage was legal, and then we saw
A huge uprising of acceptance around the world
That shows the path to equality will soon unfold

Even among the straight community
People stand up for equal opportunity
With so many influential celebrities
Who make the mark that leads us to unity

It's just so great to see understanding
And this crazy world is still withstanding
That love is love and our future is landing
In the hands of equal people!
And although it will be very hard work,
Lives of LGBT people will start to perk
And while there are places where this is the opposite
People shouldn't be afraid to come out of the closet.

And I have so much more to say,
But when we sit down at the end of the day,
We are all humans, and so we say

If I am born gay, I'm here to stay,
If I am born straight, I refuse to hate,
No matter if I feel like a girl or a boy,
We all come together with music we enjoy.

Baran Kayman

An interview about stereotypes with a gay person

Question 1: What stereotypes do people have of you?

They think that gay men act like women – that doesn't mean they are gay. For example, women like doing their hair, so just because I like to spend a lot of time doing mine, they think that I am like a girl. They think that we don't have abilities in sport. They think I'm rubbish at football, handball, rugby and basketball. They think I should do gymnastics or play netball.

They called me weak, they think I am a girl. They think that I like pink or purple – they think that I need to like pink. They call me all sorts of nasty names that I would not repeat to anyone. There are too many names to think of.

Question 2: How do you feel when people say these things to you?

I feel like I can throw them out of the window or tell them to stop saying the things that hurt me. I feel wretched and dejected, which will make me furious.

They think it's true but it's not and I know it isn't true. It is annoying and they never stop saying that. They do it all the time and I feel like I can't escape. It stays in my head after school and in my own time.

Question 3: What do these people not know about you?

They don't know all about me. I like football, basketball and lastly handball. They think I am weak but I am not weak but they don't know how much it hurts me.

Question 4: Why do you think people think of you like this?

It is like Chinese Whispers. They tell lies to other people and it builds up. They have no idea what it is like to be gay and I think they are afraid of the difference. It takes people a lot of time to get used to the difference.

Question 5: What difference do these labels make?

It makes a big difference but it shouldn't. Tom Daley is gay but he is amazing at diving. He had to suffer the same issues as me and still has managed to be the best diver in the world. I think he used all of his bad experiences to make himself better than those people. But he should not have to put up with those bad experiences to begin with. He has proven all of those people wrong, all of their stereotypes and ideas of him are wrong. Other people can't use this to find strength and they should not have to put up with it.

    I am more than the label they give me. If they took the time to get to know me then they will find it out.

Gabriel Devlin

Behind the Label

I know a little bit about how people in the LGBT community can be judged as my Aunt Sophie is a lesbian. She married when she was young, a man called Paul, and they had two sons, Nat and Josh. They were happy, but when Sophie reached the age of thirty she realised that something was not quite right and she wasn't heterosexual after all but she was a lesbian. She broke up with her husband and fell in love with a woman who she has now been with for over fifteen years. They have a really wonderful relationships but it hasn't all been easy. Although both of their families supported them and what they had done, there were lots of people who did not like it. Some of these people were strangers, and that didn't matter so much. But some of the people that disagreed were old friends and that was much worse. I don't know why this happened, but I think sometimes it's because people feel threatened in some way and they don't like people being different.

Funnily enough they lived in a small village in Gloucestershire where they were the only gay people and you would think that might be a problem. But actually they were all really cool with it and Sophie and her partner were very popular. They have had, since their meeting, three marriages to each other. The first two were just civil partnerships, but recently it has become legal for gay people to get married just like heterosexual people, so they have been able to have wedding number three! This was very important to them as it made them feel that they were officially seen to be a couple by the country and the government. I think this is a good thing as well because it should not make a difference in what you believe is right for you.

There were times when Sophie first realised that she was gay that she thought she might not tell anybody or do anything about it as she knew that life would be a lot more difficult, not just for her, but for her family as well. There is a lot of homophobia all over the world that affects all ages of people in the

More Than!

LGBT community. It can make those people very unhappy and even commit suicide. But Sophie felt that she had to be honest and be strong no matter what the response was to her coming out. There was also a risk that her work as an actor could suffer because there is a lot of prejudice even in the acting world. But that didn't stop her either. Thankfully, though, she still got lots of work once she told everyone she was gay.

It's so bad that people can be judged for anything about themselves including your sexuality. It shouldn't make any difference to anyone or how they think about you. And things have got better in the last twenty years – thanks to people like my Aunt Sophie – but there is still a long way to go before everyone socially accepts people's sexuality, whatever it is.

Ayse Atun

My name is a label, a tag. Something we humans have invented. However, names don't say who we are, or what we are for that matter. Our own actions sometimes don't even tell us who we are. As humans we have made the simple complicated. It is almost as if we have created these limits because they are easier to take; because of our fear of the unknown, of the superior. It is actually quite ridiculous that something as simple as fear shapes the world we live in. However, that may be how simple the theory behind a world of immense power may be. Because it's easier if we know what's going to happen, if we have control, if we have limits.

Our eyes should speak for ourselves and define who we really are deep within. The purity we hold within ourselves is unique. Everything in us can be fooled by the lies, the labels we have made ourselves believe. However, our eyes lead us almost like a pathway to this light concealed that is waiting for us to realise. Realise who we really are; waiting for us to realise the power that is held, that needs to gain control over us. So that the being we really are is torn from this shell plastered on from accepting the label which covers us. Eyes are a window being led from deep without ourselves, our confined secrets that tell us who we are, the centre, the cover of our surfaces.

I see a human to be happy. Not because of the way the complicated theories suggest of one logically being happy if things are going well or it's their birthday, or the way one's several muscles are forming a curve with their lips. No, because of the way this person's eyes light up and the way they have some sort of light, brightness in them. The way they have this small amount of joy and they let it grow and take them over. The way this innocent, childlike voice passionately lets the happiness overwhelm them so that in the end it has to be let out somehow, and that is with their lips crying with joy and a shrill of laughter so passionate.

We still take people for the skins that cover their hearts, before even discovering our lost selves. People tend to hide

More Than!

their true selves even from the inside, let alone what they seem like on the outside. A label may seem like the truth. However, people are more than labels given to them; they are flesh and blood, the innocence that is kept guarded within themselves. No matter what there is, there is always something else there, only it is hidden from the surface. Valuable to show.

Fletcher Adams

Patrick's Story

It all started on a dreary day, nothing different. Really normal London weather. It's Valentine's Day today and I invited Ash over so we could play with my new kittens. Anyway, my name's Patrick, or Patch as people call me. I'm gay. I haven't told my parents yet or anything though, because they think gay people are stupid people who have no concept of the world. They might not take me seriously. They started asking me today whether I had a valentine. I didn't know what to tell them so I said, 'No.' There is a kid in school who I like, but I'm scared if anyone finds out they will stop being my friends and will not hang out with me. That would be really depressing and I would have to move schools.

Maybe I should pretend to fancy Ash.

I trust Ash and we have known each other since we were really little. I could maybe tell her, see if she could help me.

I woke up this morning feeling slightly relieved that I might be able to tell someone who could see my problem from a different perspective and maybe be able to fix it. I decided to text her and ask if she wanted to go to the park as I had something to tell her. When we got to the park I told her my problem and she was quiet for a while, thinking. She finally said to tell my parents and, if they did not believe me, we could run away. I liked the idea of running away, leaving all of our troubles behind us, as Ash's parents always fought and she had a number of scars and bruises from where her parents had hit her.

When I got home I asked my mum if I could speak to her about something. She said, 'Okay, darling.'

So I told her how I didn't like girls in the same way I like boys and that I was gay. She smiled at me and then said, 'I'm so happy for you that you came out! I can't wait until I tell Dad.'

'Well, about that, Mum,' I answered. 'Does Dad really have to know? I mean, isn't he a bit homophobic?'

More Than!

'Darling,' my mum relied, 'your dad is the least homophobic person I know. He had two dads. He was adopted, you see. He has been fighting against homophobia for years.'

'But what about when I overhead you and Dad saying that gay people are stupid and have no concept of the world?'

'Patch, when did you hear this?'

'Last week, the day after school finished.'

'Sweet pea, that was when your Dad and I were talking about someone that your father works with. He was telling me what this man thought gay people were, and he and your father got into a bit of an argument.'

'So it's okay that I'm gay?' I said.

'Of course it is, darling,' my mother answered.

Connie Lammiman

Change

It's funny isn't it, how the world continues to turn? When life brings others tragedy, pain, loss, the ability to suffer, the ability to hurt.

When you are collapsing, unable to live in the body you are currently in, simply because that person isn't who you feel you are... you feel inhuman, odd.

No one knows how you feel, you can't tell anyone. They might turn you down, be as ashamed as you already are, disgusted.

But one day all the feelings, all the hurt, all the anger screams and pushes to be free – escape. Be free from the shell, the body like a hermit crab finally deciding to emerge from its refuge, after waiting until it is no longer afraid.

Numbness.

There's a stage where the whole of your body freezes, nothing can be felt. You've blurted out everything you possibly can, released every bit of carbon dioxide from your lungs. Replenished, that's the word. You feel replenished. Brand new. After knowing you are on the right path to becoming what you've always felt you must become.

My name is Kate. I'm thirty years of age and I am living a new life. I finally feel who I am; I have confidence, self-belief, freedom and space. Although, like every person, that isn't always the case. I am still that shy, self-conscious, hidden person. It is tricky becoming another, leading a completely new life that you know will throw you some even bumpier rides.

My job is what you might classify as 'normal' – working in a bar... but... I like to dance when serving the customer a pint of beer. I have become obsessed with men – some might see the remains of who I once was? However, I guess I have always wanted to be noticed differently. I've always felt a pull towards wearing long, floaty dresses and bright red lipstick, with my thick, curly brown hair shining even in the dimmest of light.

More Than!

I'm leading a life I would have dreamt about ten years ago. Perhaps, only perhaps, I feel more human.

Walking down the street feels... different. I often get a full 'eye scan' by others when they walk past me. That affects my confidence. That forces my anxiety to pump through my veins faster. I worry that perhaps they aren't seeing who I want them to see. Perhaps they are seeing who I was born as. I can't change who I once was, but I can change who I am now – if I feel that person is ME, my identity. I AM normal, just different. Aren't we all?

I was lucky to escape the closing walls within my mind, the type of walls to slowly but surely collapse day by day until they mould into your brain and form a clump of depression, worry, anxiety. I was lucky.

Life isn't easy and it never will be. Expect the Spanish Inquisition, expect your life to change. But don't ever stay a person you are not, because without your identity, without your personality, you can't be who you truly are. You.

Deniz Aydin

Throughout history there has always been stereotyping and discrimination, from Hitler's Holocaust to modern day homophobia. However, times are changing and some people believe that the future will be free of these things.

In the past these horrors were widely acceptable. An extreme example would be the Holocaust, where Hitler decided that all Jews, gays and disabled people should be killed to create the 'perfect race'. Also, in the UK, until 1967 gay men were prosecuted for their sexual preferences.

Having said that, recently LGBT people from different backgrounds and minorities appear to be more accepted, especially in developing countries. Films like *Pride* and *Selma* talk about the struggle for gay and black rights. It seems shocking nowadays that just 50 years ago people like Alan Turing were being punished to the point of suicide in our country for being gay. As well as that, in response to the French and Danish attacks, people from all faiths marched through London celebrating diversity and peace. On the 13th of March 2014, gay marriage was finally legalised in the UK, allowing many LGBT couples to get married. It does seem that things are better than they used to be.

But many people are wondering why there are still so many attacks on Jews, black people and gays. For example, incidents in Paris and Copenhagen shocked the world, and so do the beheadings of hostages by ISIS. Just a few days ago a black man trying to get on the Paris Metro was pushed away from the train by Chelsea supporters singing a racist chant. Some countries still have laws that punish people for being gay.

The word 'gay' is unfortunately still used as an insult and joke. I have experienced being called 'gay' because of the shoes I wore in Primary School, but at the time I didn't mind. However, it made me worry about being called names like that because of what I wear or how I act. It is used as an instrument for bullies to make fun of people, regardless of whether or not the person is actually gay. People are doing their best to educate out these stereotypes in any way possible, but it is still

More Than!

going on.

All over the world, people are becoming more open to those of different faiths or backgrounds. At our school, we have black history month, LGBT week and anti-bullying fortnight to celebrate this, although many people think more needs to be done to eradicate stereotyping. I believe that, despite all this effort, it will always exist. But at the very least we can make sure that it isn't used as a tool for bullying. People need to not be ignorant and think about the person behind the label as well.

Mia Truman

How nice it is to be me,
If only others could see
There is no difference between them and me

How to come out I do not know,
There is no one to talk to,
No one to say
It is OK

And that's what I wrote in my diary as I sat
On the bench in the beautiful park surrounded by
Flowers.

Why do I feel so grey?
A massive cloud over my head
On such a lovely day,
There is nothing wrong with being gay.

How will I tell my parents
Friends
And family?
What will they think?
What will they say?

This is the only way I can express my opinions:
By writing them in my diary.

At least it's not as bad as way back in the day,
When Oscar Wilde and Alan Turing
Came out.

Oscar Wilde was one of the greatest writers and
Alan Turing helped crack so many codes during the
War. They contributed so much to society but just
Because they loved the same gender they were
Treated like aliens.

More Than!

No one should ever be treated that way.

Have you ever heard of section 28?
That you should not promote homosexuality?
Well in 2003 it was abolished,
But the Conservatives were astonished,
It was Labour that said no,
It had to go!

Why is there so much hatred
For people who look exactly the same as the person
Walking past?

I don't think they understand
Would they ever imagine how it feels
To fight for the right to love who you love?

I have decided that it's time to let my parents know,
I am leaving the safety of my park bench,
I wonder what they are going to say
Well, they are my parents and they love me.
Nothing bad is going to happen.

I can't even imagine how it would feel if you told
Someone and then you got put in prison.

I have done it!
My parents were fine about it!
I am so glad to be living in these days.

If only other people would understand the difficulty
Of it all, and we could bring back the lives of people
Who have suffered, unlike me

Everyone used to disapprove of homosexuality,
But that was years ago
We are here now
And some people still disapprove of it
So why don't you help someone out today

More Than!

People fuss over silly things like this that don't
Matter when they should be worrying about much
Bigger things like the war in Russia

Russia is basically like the UK but in the 1900s
Because they are at war and it is illegal there to be
Lesbian, gay, bisexual and transgender.

Kate Hyatt

A day in my life is like a life in one day.

Getting up in the morning is the hardest part of anyone's day, autistic or not, but getting dressed is not as hard as you might think. I struggle with buttons because my fingers find it complicated so I normally use Velcro. For breakfast I have toast and juice. I learned to say juice ten years ago. It sounds like 'yoos' to most people but if you know me well it makes sense. Then my key worker comes to pick me up.

Outside I sometimes meet my neighbours who can only see my skin. Normally the first thing I hear is, 'The Lord did not create people that colour, it's the devil's work.' I have lived with it for the past twenty-one years. I am mixed race. Along with being called spaz and retard, I am called nigger by not only white people, but also other black people who tell me I am not worthy of being black because of my disability. I prefer what my cousin says – she reads *Mr Men* books with me and tells me I am Mr Beautiful.

The walk down my road with my key worker goes past the corner-shop where there is a gang of white kids. They jeer and shout abuse. They call me retard. I just wish I could tell them, 'No, I'm not a retard, I'm autistic.' I find it hard to communicate with other people. When people see me they automatically label me as disabled and nothing else. They don't put in the time to get to know the real me.

When I was a baby I used to scream whenever someone came near me. I thought touch was anger. I have grown to no longer fear being touched but it is still not a sensation I enjoy.

A lot of people think that because of my disability my brain doesn't work properly but it actually works just like yours. I still have thoughts and ideas but I can't communicate them. You cannot understand the frustration of not being able to explain myself! I could be the next Einstein but no-one would know because I can't talk about things like you can.

Next I have to walk through the park, which in many ways may be worse than walking down my road. This is mainly because of all the pitying looks I get from people walking past

More Than!

me. My route takes me past the playground where the smaller children ask, 'Mum, why is he walking like that?'

I don't mind so much when the mum tells them the straight answer, but when the parent ushers them away as if it's contagious, that's the worst part of my day. The look of disgust you get is enough to kill you.

Next I go to my college. My college specialises in people like me – good someone does! There they teach me all the skills I need to know to live with me. They taught me how to say juice. They also have weekly sessions that help me to grip things better.

Then it's back through the park but it's later and there aren't so many people. Normally when I get back next door have gone inside, but the gang is still there shouting racial abuse.

My labels are black and autistic. I call myself Daniel.

Inspired by my cousin.

Ceren Bektas

Friday afternoon. YESSSSSS!!! Two whole days playing football and fighting with my little brother.

'Let's go shopping tomorrow!' exclaimed Laura. My thought crashed on the floor.

'Omg definitely!' 'Amazing idea!' 'Oh yes!' chanted all the other girls. I just stood there, my face crumpled.

'Is that a yes, Lily?' asked Laura

'Umm, well actually...'

'Great! Okay girls, be here at one tomorrow. It's going to be so fun!'

She skipped away, laughing and singing, swaying her arms. All the other girls chased after her. I hate how Laura can just control everything, and everyone always has to agree. I crossed the road and headed home. Another weekend ruined.

As soon as I opened the front door I ran to my room and changed out of my disgusting clothes into my cosy tracksuit and an Arsenal top. Charlotte had done this complicated braid thing all over my hair and it looked ridiculous. I yanked it out and tied it in a classic ponytail, the way I like it. I looked at my face in the mirror. Ugh. What was it with all this makeup? My face is not a colouring book. I washed it all off and lay on my bed, sorting out my Match Attax cards. A few minutes later my best friend Dave walked in, a ball under his arm.

'Yo Lily, come outside! We're playing a match and we need you!'

I leapt off my bed and rushed outside. If any of the girls saw me now they would've thought that I was mad. Maybe I was.

Laura's house was basically 'every girl's dream' as people would say. The walls were soft pink, with pictures of her and her friends all in pretty pink and flowery frames. She had a huge white desk placed right next to her purple king-sized bed, coated with millions of cushions. Her desk had all her makeup and perfume, probably worth hundreds of tickets to football matches. My room had plain, dark-blue walls, a small single bed, and a tiny black wardrobe, and that was it. I didn't have a desk so I'd just stuff all my bits and pieces in this little box I

More Than!

stole from my brother. But this was my room and that's how I liked it.

The next day I did it: I did what I didn't have the courage to do ever before. Instead of wearing my pink designer dress, I wore my favourite baggy jeans with a plain jumper. I tied my hair in my favourite ponytail and didn't bother with any makeup. When I got there all the girls gave the reaction I knew was coming.

'Omg! What the HELL are you wearing?!!? And what did you do with your hair, it looks awful! You didn't even bother to put on any makeup!'

I smiled at the girls carelessly. 'I couldn't care less about what you think about me right now. This is who I am, who I always was, and I'm not going to change for you guys'.

I gave them a last glance, turned my back on them, and marched into JD.

Louis Brine

Mike ran into the fire station for the beginning of his shift. He was working nights, and his colleagues were sat around talking and joking, waiting for a call-out. In the background the television was on.

'Did you see the game last night?' asked Isaac, one of his mates at the station.

'Yeah, it was a great match wasn't it?' replied Mike. 'Especially the Sanchez goal. We made Chelsea look like a bunch of sissies.'

He directed this to Ross, the only Chelsea fan there. There was laughter as they enjoyed the banter.

They turned their attention to the television. Alan Carr's *Chatty Man* was on.

'Turn it over,' said Ross. 'We don't want to watch that camp poof: my mum's tougher than him.'

'Can you imagine if we had a 'gay' working here?' said Isaac.

'At least the place would be spotless!' joked Ross.

A loud bang stopped their laughter, then the call came in. There had been a bomb in a pub in Dalston, a couple of streets away. A few moments later three fire-engines left the station – they were on their way.

Mike was pumped up, adrenalin flowing through his body. He loved the rush and excitement of call-outs. He was ready to take on anything.

When they reached the scene no-one was quite prepared for the horror in front of them. A man ran past screaming and there were body-parts strewn all over the place. The front of the building had been blown away, there were fires burning and desperate calls for help. There was a huge crater where tables had once been.

Mike turned to Isaac, his superior, to get instructions but found him vomiting by the side of the truck. Mike stepped up and barked out instructions to the rest of the crew.

'There's a group of people trapped inside, but it's too dangerous to get them out – the ceiling's about the collapse,' shouted Ross.

More Than!

'Okay, I'm on it!' screamed Mike.
'No! It's too risky.'
But Mike didn't listen: he ran in.
There were three people trapped by a fallen beam. Above them was another beam balancing precariously.
'Don't worry – you'll be fine. I'm going to get you out.'
He managed to lift the beam enough to free two of them but the third was completely stuck.
'It's going to go, Mike!' yelled Ross.
With one last, huge effort, he managed to free the man, and as he dragged him to safety the beam crashed down and landed exactly where they had been.
Mike was the hero of the night.
They went back to the station, cleaned up and got ready to go home.
'See you tomorrow, Mike,' said Isaac. 'You were amazing tonight, a real asset to our crew!'
Once home, Mike opened the door to find the table set for breakfast. There was a card and red roses. He saw the smiling face of his boyfriend Paul, who greeted him with a kiss.
'Happy Valentine's Day, Mike,' he said.

Thomas O'Shea

Billy wandered into school, not responding to the vile comments his fellow pupils shouted.

'Silly Billy!'

'Bonkers Billy!'

These were just a few of the insults other children named him. Billy suffered from severe learning difficulties. He could hardly read or write and he barely knew his multiples from 1 to 5. School was torture for him. The kids pulled faces and mouthed names to each other while the teacher struggled to help Billy. At break-times he would take refuge in the toilet cubicles and read books to pass the time. The only time that Billy was ever happy was in the pool.

Billy was an excellent swimmer and his coach was working him for a place on the upcoming Paralympic GB team. It was tough but Billy truly enjoyed it. It was his getaway from life, and during that brief hour and a half in the pool he forgot all his problems.

Billy sat in Geography being bombarded with paper balls, thinking of tomorrow. It was his one chance for a place on the team. It was what he and his coach had been waiting for. His daydreaming was interrupted by a pen-lid in the eye. Filled with utter contempt and rage he swung a punch blindly at the boy who threw the lid at him. Blood was gushing freely out of the boy's nose and onto the carpet. Billy didn't have any parents to be sent for so was sent straight home as the Head couldn't care less. He decided to get an early night in preparation for tomorrow.

It was his time to shine. He was ready. And he was off! It was a sloppy start and he would have to make up for it fast. Half done and he was 5th, closing down on 4th. All of a sudden a thought went through his head. All the jeering kids cursing him, shouting abuse at him. How good it would be to show them. So Billy powered through, his muscles screaming to stop, but he stayed strong and persisted. Then it was over and he waited anxiously for the result to pop up. It read 'Billy Brown – 1st'!

More Than!

The school had gathered for an emergency assembly today. The Head took the microphone and began to speak.

'Children, this is an incredibly successful school. We never fail to achieve, but until today we have never had a greater sporting achievement.'

Everybody turned their heads to a student who was known for running the fastest 100m in the school. He smiled in arrogance.

'Can Billy Brown please stand up, and everyone else put your hands together for the school's first Paralympian ever.'

For a moment there was a deafening silence. But slowly the school began to clap and then erupted with shouts and cheers of pride. Billy had never been so happy.

Lily McKay

My Brother, Isaac

You lay tight, curled up underneath dozens of blankets. Giggles swirled into my ears as I ran round and round your little homemade cradle.

'Stoooppppp,' you cried as I tickled you. 'Pleeeeeasee. Please no, Kitty, it tickles!'

'That's the whole point, silly,' I replied as you tried weakly to push my hands away. Impossible though, during a laughing fit.

Once a joyous little boy. Where are you now? My little Isaac. Gone. Hidden beneath layers and layers of black bruises.

I was at least pleased to see your heart-rate completely normal on the ECG.

'He's recovering,' the doctors said. But too sad, I denied it in my head. But aloud I tried to seem relieved.

'All is well,' I supposedly agreed.

A peaceful little thing you were, though completely oblivious of me standing next to you. At first I was scared, all the wires running from various machines, but I then realised I was not the injured one. You lay like a new-born baby sleeping its first night's sleep. Yet you didn't sleep for one night, it was day after day after day. Home to school to hospital to home every day. For you. I never for one minute regretted it. I never ever regretted seeing you, sitting next to you, waiting for you to move, for you to wake.

Mum called, telling us dinner was ready, finally releasing you from my tickle trap. You lay, your arms and legs flung on the floor. We both sat together, staring at the bland ceiling above us.

You took a deep breath, we stood, and I brushed you down. I remember you wore beautiful pinstriped corduroys and a blue denim shirt. You had an amazing sense of style, unique but 'absolutely fabulous' you'd say.

One day I recall, I was more scared than ever before when the police rushed in. They found the boys, the crooks that put you here. The mean, ignorant, homophobic bullies that put my

More Than!

brother to such harm. I was angry – no, furious. I screamed. This was supposed to be a good moment. But instead my rage controlled my body, wanting to have a word with these 'boys'. I ran and ran. Endless hospital corridors seemed to calm me down. I was relaxed. Relaxed like you.

You'd spend many hours a weekend sat under the kitchen table cutting up mum's fashion magazines, creating 'Isaac's fashion events'. I miss those Sundays. I miss you. The way you'd bunk with me when the nightmares stole your dreams. The way you'd pronounce the word 'fabulous' – fabbb-u-lice. I loved my brother, I loved you. But now you're gone. Forever.

Ciar Wild

STEREOTYPES

STEREOTYPES ARE PAINTED ACROSS THE WORLD,
THESE LIES ARE ALWAYS TWISTED AND CURLED,
YOU SHOULDN'T BELIEVE THEM, ONLY TINY PARTS ARE TRUE,
ALL TEACHERS DRINK COFFEE? NO, BUT SOME DO.

THEY CAN BE HOMOPHOBIC AND RACIST,
ABOUT RELIGION OR SEXIST,
THEY AFFECT MANY PEOPLE'S LIVES,
FROM BLACK TO WHITE TO GIRLS TO GUYS.

AGAINST TRANSGENDER,
AS WELL AS LESBIAN AND GAY,
ALSO BISEXUAL,
IT'S NOT AN INSULT TO SAY

IT'S BAD ENOUGH NOW,
IN THE WORLD THAT WE LIVE IN
SO DON'T PREACH STEREOTYPES,
THEY'RE THE WORST SIN.

LESBIAN AND GAY

DON'T BE ASHAMED TO SAY,
IF YOU'RE A HOMOSEXUAL,
SINCE 1 IN 5 PEOPLE ARE LESBIAN OR GAY

PEOPLE SAY GAY IS A MAN WHO IS SASSY,
WHO WEARS DIFFERENT CLOTHES IN PINK,
BUT THEY'RE ONLY THE SLIGHTEST BIT DIFFERENT FROM YOU AND ME,
AND THAT'S HOW THEY SEXUALLY THINK.

GAY MEANS HAPPY AND IT'S CHANGED OVER TIME,

More Than!

TO AN INSULT AT ANYONE AT ALL,
IT'S STUPID I KNOW BUT THAT'S WHAT'S HAPPENING,
SO WE'VE GOT TO FIGHT IT AND STAND OR WE'LL FALL.

DON'T BE ASHAMED TO SAY,
IF YOU'RE A HOMOSEXUAL,
SINCE 1 IN 5 PEOPLE ARE LESBIAN OR GAY

'LESBO' MEANS LESBIAN,
IN A MUCH RUDER WAY,
IT'S NOW AN INSULT OR JOKE,
SAID JUST LIKE 'YOU'RE GAY'.

THEY WERE CALLED PERVERTS,
AND ALL KINDS OF NAMES,
BUT THEY STOOD AND FOUGHT FOR THEMSELVES,
THE LESBIANS AND GAYS

DON'T BE ASHAMED TO SAY
IF YOU'RE A HOMOSEXUAL,
SINCE 1 IN 5 PEOPLE ARE LESBIAN OR GAY

IT'S IN NO WAY UNUSUAL,
IT'S NOT A JOKE IT'S FORMAL,
THEY AREN'T SASSY OR MANLY,
THEY'RE ORDINARY, THEY'RE NORMAL.

SO BEFORE YOU SAY THAT GAYS ARE GIRLY,
THINK, ARE THEY REALLY?
OR YOU SAY LESBIANS ARE MANLY,
THINK, AM I THINKING CLEARLY?

DON'T BE ASHAMED TO SAY,
IF YOU'RE HOMOSEXUAL,
SINCE 1 IN 5 ARE LESBIAN OR GAY

SEXISM

WHY ARE MEN MORE BEFITTED,

More Than!

THAN WOMEN BY MUCH, MUCH MORE,
BIGGER PAY AND BETTER JOBS,
IT'S NOT FAIR AT ALL.

WOMEN ARE TOLD THAT THEY'RE USELESS,
EVEN THOUGH THEY PROVIDE ALL OF THE FOOD,
THEY DO ALL THE HOUSEWORK AND LOOK AFTER CHILDREN,
AND YET FROM WORK THEY ARE SHOOED.

IN STORIES THEY'RE WEAK,
ALL WAYS IN NEED OF A SAVIOUR,
A DAMSEL IN DISTRESS,
THOUGH IT'S THEM WHO GO INTO LABOUR.

WHY ARE MEN MORE BEFITTED,
THAN WOMEN BY MUCH, MUCH MORE
BIGGER PAY AND BETTER JOBS,
IT'S NOT FAIR AT ALL.

LIFE FOR WOMEN IS MORE OF A CHALLENGE,
THEY STILL CAN'T GET JOBS OR VOTE,
IN SYRIA THEY CAN'T DRIVE CARS,
BUT OF THEIR COMPASSION THEY CAN GLOAT.

WHY DO WE SAY HU**MAN**S,
ALTHOUGH WOMEN GIVE BIRTH TO OUR KIN,
WHAT ABOUT THE FEMALES,
OR DID THAT IDEA GO INTO THE BIN?

WHY ARE MEN MORE BEFITTED,
THAN WOMEN BY MUCH, MUCH MORE
BIGGER PAY AND BETTER JOBS,
IT'S NOT FAIR AT ALL.

IT'S BAD ENOUGH NOW,
IN THE WORLD THAT WE LIVE IN,
SO DON'T PREACH STEREOTYPES,
THEY'RE THE WORST SIN.

Lyra Robinson-Winning

Life Story Not Label

To think about equality and diversity, I chose to interview my godmother's partner, Lil. Lil is a black gay woman in her 50s, who grew up in London. I have known her all my life. In the interview I learnt things about Lil's life that I had never known, particular how hard it was to grow up in a less equal society than we have nowadays.

Lyra: How do you define your identity?

Lil: I am a black woman who happens to be gay. I am of Afro-Caribbean origin but I was brought up in London. I went to school here so most of my identity has been formed here in the capital.

Lyra: Are there any parts of your identity that you sometimes feel you can't talk about with other people?

Lil: No, I'm always having a bash at it! Recently there's been a lot of issues around immigration in this country, and I get angry because I remember when we were children there were the issues around no blacks, no Irish, no gays, and that was heavy for me growing up in the '70s. Mum was a nurse, Dad was a train-driver, and they were like the new emerging black middle class. We lived in a private road. We were the only black people there and I know we used to get looked at through the windows, but that was '70s Britain – it wasn't a nice era. But in today's twenty-first century, I try and challenge it as much as I can. I don't tolerate it. Those days are done, from the '70s until now.

Lyra: Is there anyone else in your family that shares the same identity?

More Than!

Lil: My cousin. He's a gay man and he's very into gay rights and he's married to a white person but he sticks to his own beliefs. He eats black food and likes to go to the nice places. He likes all the soul music, but all these things are stereotypes – but he rises above it all and likes to be himself. Anyone challenges him, he challenges them back: 'I'm a black man. I'm a gay man. You can't tell me how to behave to how to live or what to do. This is my life and my identity.'

Lyra: Is it important to you to see your identity in films, TV programmes and books?

Lil: I remember in the '70s, on the TV they used to have programmes like *It Ain't Half Hot Mum*, they were very anti-black to be honest. Today we would call them racist; they didn't have any black imagery in them whatsoever. Well, they had a black character but he was abused in it. We've moved on now. You get a few lead characters in film today but there needs to be more. It is important that black people have images they can aspire to. It's crucial.

Lyra: How would you feel if certain parts of your identity were against the law in this country?

Lil: We used to have something called 'stop and search'. If you have 10 people, 7 black, 3 white, you can guarantee that the 7 black people will get stopped and the 3 white people will get let go by the police. The Home Secretary has recently decided to ban the 'stop and search' business because she says you can't judge people by their colour. But people do. If you look at the prison population you'll find that the vast majority are black, so that speaks volumes about the law: it doesn't really protect.

Zoe Edwards

It's early Monday morning in January and I trudge down the stairs with my Ugg boots on. I open the front door and step into the bustling high street, the sun shining through the trees.

Face in a book, pushing his glasses up his nose, comes a stubbly-faced, pink-haired 'nerd', stumbling past me. He mutters, 'Sorry,' and I dodge round him. I look away in annoyance and imagine him going home to switch his book for a computer screen.

Swinging my bag, I walk down the street and into the local grocer's and take a place in the queue. I wait for ages and when it's my turn a tall, well-dressed woman pushes me aside with her handbag and shouts her order. As she leaves, I push her slightly... Out of the corner of my eye I see her wipe her coat where I just made contact. This woman has 'issues' I think to myself.

I head back, not concentrating, and fall into an ancient man dressed in a pink dress, leggings, ballet pumps and a headband. He exclaims, 'I am so sorry,' in an embarrassed voice. I nod back in dismissal. Blushing, I hurry on, sneaking a look back at the man, who I presume is transgender.

Near the end of the road I enter my grandmother's shabby, unkempt home to hear a shout of, 'Sam, is that you?' Biting my tongue I mutter back, 'Yes.' Rubbing my tired eyes, I head into her 'old person', foul-smelling living room. The blinds are shut, the fire is off and so are the lights, TV and radiator.

'Gran,' I yell, 'you'll get pneumonia!'

She just shrugs in reply and smiles. 'Sammy, you are always so suspicious, try and relax.'

Suddenly my brother Peeta appears at the top of the stairs. He comes down and clasps me in a bear hug, and I say, 'What have you been doing?'

He grins. 'Xbox.'

I sigh. 'You'll get a headache or square eyes.'

Peeta pouts, 'You're exactly what Gran said – "suspicious".'

I glare at him and Gran and storm out fuming.

I walk fast trying to calm myself and enter the park. There

More Than!

are lots of pink flags, it's really busy, and I see that it's a Community Fun Run for a cancer charity. At the starting post is the ancient man in the dress who I'd collided with. I feel embarrassed and slightly annoyed with myself that I assumed that he was transgender.

I look around and I see the 'nerd' with pink hair sprinting with the top athletes and I wished I had thought better of him.

Close to the finish I see the rude woman from the grocer's dishing out oranges to the runners and cheering them on. I see a dirty mark on her sleeve.

Perhaps my brother is right and I should not be so judgemental. I think to myself that there is so much more to people than first impressions. Never judge a book by its cover.

Servican Yeter

I am going to start with a question. Do you think that gay or lesbian people have equal rights like us? Yes or no? I think yes because they are humans as well, it's just that they like people of their own gender.

I wonder how gay and lesbian people feel because people always curse them just because they are gay or lesbian. They probably feel like they need to move schools because every day they feel sad because people upset them.

What would you do if you were in their shoes? You would feel upset and angry. So If I was you I would stop bullying gay or lesbian people.

Some gay and lesbian people get home-schooled because people bully them badly. Some gay and lesbian people don't tell their parents because people threaten them.

Being gay and lesbian is the same as having a right to an education because they are both human rights. Ones that treat everyone with respect no matter what they are, and have the right to go to school.

Just because people are gay or lesbian it does not mean that they cannot fulfil their lives. So if they want to be a scientist they can, if they get good grades.

People probably pray to God to ask him, 'Why did you make me gay or lesbian?' because they are not proud of who they are.

If people bully you, just tell a teacher. Do not try and attack the person or you will be excluded. You can trust an adult to sort out the problem.

Violence is never the answer. If you attack someone on the streets you will be arrested and imprisoned for maybe five years.

Some people actually like being gay or lesbian and that is perfectly fine. Why don't people try and make friends with gay or lesbian people so they don't get upset, and they would have backup when they need it.

Why can't people forget about people being gay or lesbian and just have fun?

More Than!

Being gay or lesbian is the same as being transgender, because in one you are born with it or as you grow up it happens, and the other is changing gender, so it is not fair for these people to be treated badly.

Some people have special needs and they get bullied as well but they can't help it because they have special needs. You're born with it so it's not funny. Some special needs are very bad like when children start to speak late.

Lily Crooke

The train pulls into Caledonian Road & Barnsbury and creaks to a halt. Blank-faced people look out of the grimy windows, their faces empty and bored. As soon as the doors slide open people rush out, busy and frantic to get to work, the same cycle every day. A man in grey tracksuit bottoms and the same grey faded jumper limps onto the train. His face is just as bleak as his clothes.

'Money for a man with no home. Money for a man all alone.'

The people try to ignore him as they look down into their phones and newspapers. You can see in their eyes that they know they should care but whatever they are doing is just too important to stop.

'Why should I give him my money?' they mutter. 'We've earned our money, he's probably never done a day's work in his life.'

And:

'He'll only gamble it away or spend it on drugs.'

They're desperate to find an excuse not to get involved.

But...

His name is James. He was brought up by foster-carers and had dreams of being an electrician. He worked hard on a building site for three years but couldn't continue after his leg got crushed under fallen scaffolding. From them on, his life fell apart. He lost his job, his flat and his friends. He had no-one to fall back on.

'The next stop is Highbury and Islington.'

An old lady hobbles onto the train and automatically a man offers her his seat. She smiles and gratefully accepts. She is overdressed in the cold weather with snow boots and a big duffle-coat. Her face is only just visible over at least three scarves and is partially covered by wisps of white cloud-like hair. The people sneak pitying looks from the other side of the carriage but only once she's fallen asleep.

'What a funny old woman.'

'She couldn't hurt a fly.'

'Should I wake her up? She might not be able to get back to

More Than!

wherever she wants to go if she misses her stop.'

But...

Her name is Xanthe and she is not the sweet old woman they think she is. In 1964 she opened the first karate school for girls in London, which won the Karate Awards from 1967-2004, when she finally retired aged 72. She herself reached black belt when she was 11 and had won 124 fights by the time she was 15. She is still regarded as one of the greatest karate masters every recorded.

At Canonbury a swarm of men in suits get onto the already full train. Screaming children hold on to the swaying bars, trying to keep hold. It's chaos. One man doesn't seem swayed by any of this as he sits down with his iPad in his hands. He is wearing a grey Savile Row suit and shiny black shoes that absent-mindedly tap against the grimy floor of the train. The woman opposite looks at him angrily.

'Bankers like him have all the money in the world and would never think about anyone else.'

She looks at his new iPad. It has just been released and the surface reflects the sun so the screen shines almost white. It clearly outdoes her little grey phone. She looks down in silent disgust.

But...

His name is Max and it is true that he is a banker and earns an astoundingly large amount of money a year. Although he doesn't spend it like she thinks he does. On Sundays he is a volunteer at a charity that helps people who have depressions after his brother committed suicide four years ago. He helps them to get their lives back on track. He also gives 25% of the money he earns every year to charity but likes to remain anonymous.

There were thousands of other stories like these on just that one train. Everyone has a story to tell, and most of the time their outward appearance doesn't tell it.

Leila Edelzstein

A Change of Clothes (inspired by Grayson Perry)

'Okay, I double dare you to wear your sister's dress!'

The others laugh and jeer. Should I take the dare? I inhale and slip into the tight fabric. I watch their faces contort in disbelief.

'That's so gay, Gabe!' My room explodes into roaring, boisterous guffaws. I laugh along uneasily. The group leaves a while later and I am left alone in my sister's dress, pondering what to do now. The front door opens with a dim metallic rattle and the unmistakeable sound of my sister's cropped nylon jacket creasing against itself is coming towards me. I stiffen with panic. It's too late to do anything so instead I perch on the bed of our shared room, compose myself and try to look dignified. She bursts through the door and gapes.

'Gabe, you idiot! What the hell?'

She snatches up the dress and I find myself longing to be back in its silky grip.

I stay on my side of the room all afternoon, hunched over a football magazine and skimming through my favourite players distractedly. I hear footsteps and see my mum making her way towards me. She wants to know why I was wearing my sister's dress. I shrug and say that I want to go to bed. She leaves.

That night I hardly sleep, sorting through the confused clumps of thoughts in my head. What's wrong with me? I convince myself that I was just being stupid, but the indescribable feeling I felt when wearing the dress still haunts me.

A few weeks later, after school, I pour my pocket money into a wallet and take my usual route to the newsagent's to buy the weekly football magazine, *Match*. On my way back I pass Gap. A bright red dress in the window display catches my eye and, involuntarily, I walk in. I have enough to buy the dress.

Quivering in excitement I ignore the odd look I receive from the cashier and take the dress home. I feel like a criminal loaded with taboo as I hurry back to my room. I slip into the dress and relish the air on my bare legs. Then I catch a glimpse

More Than!

of myself in my sister's mirror and my heart skips a beat. I'm a freak. At that moment my sister walks in and I feel the atmosphere tense.

'OMG! Are you a freakin' camp fairy or something?' She walks out and the door slams.

I skip dinner and bury myself in the duvet. I'm not gay, I don't know what I am but it's not that. I have a crush on Betty Smith at school so I can't be. Tears sting my eyes and dribble away.

I hardly sleep that night. The next morning my body climbs into the red dress of its own accord and I know it's crazy but I walk downstairs and smile at everyone. My dad leans back in his chair and shoots me a broad, supportive smile. Yes, I am a transvestite but I am not gay. I am also a brother and a son. I am Gabe.

Louis Powell

Tembo

In a small village, somewhere in Africa, there lived an elephant called Tembo. Elephants were big and clumsy, (well, that was the feeling of all the other animals in the village). Tembo was sick and tired of being seen this way. The hyena always smirked when Tembo lumbered past on his way to painting class. The gazelles would guffaw when he attempted to run.

Tembo had had enough. He wanted to go to the city and become a surgeon. This required skill, precision and a very steady hand – not something which elephants were known for.

Tembo was determined. He told his family and friends that he was going to go to the big city to make his dreams come true. His parents were concerned. They knew the sort of prejudice that Tembo would be up against. Elephants weren't wanted in the city; they took up too much space and were seen as a burden amongst city-dwellers. The successful animals that had carved out important careers in the city tended to be the lean, quick movers and shakers. How would an elephant like Tembo survive in this kind of environment? Time would soon tell.

As Tembo left his home village he was filled with anticipation and excitement, as well as some trepidation.

He arrived to the smells and sounds of the city, and wasted no time in finding out where the local hospitals were. As he wandered around he could see people tutting and remarking, even though he was being careful not to get in anyone's way. Some were even pointing. Not many elephants came into the city: this was a rare sight.

Tembo entered the hospital and he saw a wall of eyes staring at him. He bounded towards the front desk and asked to speak to the animal in charge.

'What's it regarding?' was the response.

'I'd like to come and work here,' said Tembo. 'As a surgeon.'

There was silence followed by the loudest eruption of laughter that Tembo had ever heard. Animals were rolling around on the floor, crying with laughter. Tembo felt more embarrassed

More Than!

than he had ever been in his entire life. He wanted the ground to swallow him up.

'Are you sure? With those clumsy feet?'

'Yes, I'm sure,' replied Tembo.

'What's all the commotion?' boomed a loud, authoritative voice.

Tembo looked up and saw before him a great ape in a doctor's coat.

'And who are you?' quizzed the ape.

'This,' said the nurse, 'is an elephant who wants to be a surgeon!' She was still trying to suppress her laughter.

The Doctor looked at the elephant.

'Well, that's very commendable,' he said, 'but the journey to becoming a surgeon is a long and hard one. There is much learning to do and many skills to acquire. However, the greatest asset a surgeon can possess is a delicate touch. With respect, I have never seen an animal of your size with such a skill but I like your courage.'

Tembo was taken into the teaching theatre. Word had got around and the viewing gallery was jam-packed with bemused animals.

The doctor lead him over to the operating table where, in front of him, lay a single scalpel and a large mango. Tembo was instructed to dissect the mango and retrieve the stone inside without leaving a single mark. He picked up the scalpel with his heavy foot. The crowd gasped and lent forwards. Then Tembo passed the scalpel from his foot to his delicate trunk. In a flurry of beautiful movements and cuts, he worked over the mango skilfully. Then Tembo turned to the doctor who was standing nearby astounded, handed him the unmarked stone and smiled.

Rione Nurse

If I wasn't gay would people care?
Would they actually let me breathe the same air?
Could I actually go to school
Without people being so cruel?
Could I live in a world with no hate?
Maybe people would love me if I was straight
It's not as easy as people think.
I can't just go to a shrink.
I didn't choose to be this way
You really think I wanted to be gay?
I don't want attention, I don't want fame
This isn't some sort of game.
I am who I am and that's okay,
Sadly most people don't see it that way.
I only wish I could be the same,
To have a wedding and it not be a shame.
I want to have kids and not be judged,
I don't want my reputation to be smudged.
But apparently I'm different now,
Sick in the head somehow.
Therapy and shock treatment for something that can't be fixed,
How did I get put into this mix?
Toxic and tragic, that's my life
It's like I was stabbed in the back with a knife.
I'm gay, what's wrong with that?
I get treated like some kind of rat.
Using your holy books and religion
To fights against something that makes no difference.
I want to be human not a punching bag,
Always getting called a 'fag'.
Let that word have power and it gets to you,
But that word's as good as whatever's stuck to the bottom of

More Than!

my shoe.
I love being this way,
I don't care what you say.
You're the one insulting so many people without knowing a thing,
Because we are human just like you under the skin.
You may think you can call us names,
But you don't understand that we are all the same.
You may listen to people's negative views,
But maybe have the courage to speak to us then you might have a clue.
There are people getting hurt without even a say,
Because others hurt them and don't want them to stay.
Violence against them they don't ever play,
All because they're gay and others don't think it's okay.
Think about the ones who've been hurt and died,
And the families who've screamed and cried.
Never told a soul – 'I'm okay,' they lied,
Gave up on life because there was no place to hide.
Be aware of what you're saying before it's too late,
You might be justifying someone's hidden hate.
It's not okay to deny our rights
As this will cause a lot more fights!
Let us love each other and accept who we choose as our mate
Because life can be short so let's make a change before it's too late.
Don't stand there and treat me with pity,
If you pity me, then tell me.
If you hate me, then tell me,
Don't treat me like the lesser because I'm not
Don't treat me like I'm sick or confused
Because I'm not.
Gay doesn't mean lesser.
It doesn't mean sick and it doesn't mean confused.
It means that we are open.

Mack Quicke

Labels, what are they? Do they define us or imprison us? Are they natural and instinctive or is it just ignorance? How do you break down something like that? For instance, would you trust a woman more than a man based on appearance? Or assume that someone is gay if they dress in women's clothing? The main point is this: how does that person feel? Since this is LGBT month I will try to focus on that.

There is the problem of the gay stereotype and how you are automatically judged for being gay. People are judged on their sexuality way too much, just by the gender of the person they are attracted to. Even now reading this you may be painting a picture of a man who wears v-necks, teaches a dance class, is camp and has plucked eyebrows. All of that is just guesswork, and the assumption that if you're gay all of your traits are magically changed because of one detail. Then there would be the argument that some gay people may fit into the stereotyped moulds. However, this is not because they are gay, this is the simple fact that this is what one enjoys. It is even bad to label them as a different type of person. They are equal to you, they're no different from you, so even by labelling them as different you're just building more barriers. Then there is the other side of the coin in the person you are affecting through this labelling. For example, if a heterosexual man is camp and takes pride in his appearance, people, without any backstory, will label him as gay. Here's a story to give an example of this labelling:

'Two minutes, ladies and gentlemen, before showtime, two minutes.'

The loudspeaker crackled off. The butterflies were churning my insides apart. I'd never done a show as big as this before. Would people like it? What would they say? I put on my dress and make-up in front of a mirror surrounded by blazing lights. I slid on my crimson stilettos and the bright white wig.

I could hear the roar of the crowd on the other side of the velvet curtain. The curtain lifted and I strutted out and did my poses. The crowd started to roar with laughter. Applause and jeers were raining in from all corners. I carried on until the end of the catwalk, receiving a lot of excited noise. I spin backward and don't stop walking until I'm within touching distance of the curtain. I do a final pirouette and spin out.

As soon as I'm out of sight I start to take off my wig, revealing stubby black hair. I scratch my beard and head for the showers. Later on in the night I slip out the back exit and drive home. As soon as I open the door I see my two sons charging at me to hug me.

'What's for supper, Dad?' one says.

'Bangers and mash, son,' I say with a smile.

My wife walks in and asks, 'How'd the show go?'

'Excellent,' I say, buzzing.

The labelling of transsexual can be a difficult one because many will just assume the person is gay or even mock them. Many gays, lesbians, bisexuals, transsexuals are sometimes mocked or treated differently for the simple fact that they are LGBT. How should we go about changing this, breaking down these barriers? It's a tough subject to deal with, but breaking down these stereotypes is a good place to start.

Anisa Khatun

'Mom, I'm doing a research project on diversity. I want to know about diversity in your days!'

'Well, in my days I've been labelled as a Muslim terrorist because of the way I looked. I still remember the times when I was called a terrorist because of the stereotype that all Muslims are terrorists.'

Everyone is labelled because of the way they act, from gay, lesbian, bisexual to many other things, but is it right to label someone just because they are different?

'Well... there was this time, it was in March... it was dreadful for me. It was the first time that I was labelled and identified as a terrorist. I wore an Indian outfit with a hijab and left the house with a positive vibe. I got on the bus and people were looking at me as if I had committed a murder. The driver didn't let me go on the bus as he thought I was going to plant a bomb. I left. This is how it feels like being labelled.

'As I was walking people kept giving me dirty looks. I felt worried and it felt as if the whole world turned upside-down and I felt so suffocated. I needed a glass of water and so I went to the closest café that I could see. I went in and as soon as my body got into the café everyone looked up and stared at me and then moved away from me. I felt unwanted. Many people hurried up eating and then left. This made me sick and furious. Can't people dress and act how they want without being labelled? I went up to the counter and ordered a drink. Straight away the lady went, so I went to the far end corner of the café and sat down. I could hear people murmuring things like, 'She'll plant a bomb any moment, hurry up and get out.'

'All of a sudden a herd of police came in and came towards me and aimed their guns at me. Everyone got up and looked at me. One of the policemen told me to surrender. I was shocked. I froze. I was flabbergasted. A policewoman came towards me, searched me but found nothing. No-one helped.

'This wasn't the only time I was suspected as a 'Muslim terrorist'. There was this time when I was coming from India. I was just leaving the airport and I had lots of luggage. The police thought that it contained a bomb. The police kept looking at me, and everywhere I looked I could see policemen. There were more policemen behind me with huge dogs. I was hurrying to get out and the police thought I was trying to lose them. Out of the blue a huge-built man came in front of me, grabbed my luggage and searched it and found nothing. Dogs were sniffing me and people were looking at me.

'I was labelled as a Muslim terrorist but that doesn't affect me as I know that I'm not. Everyone is different, which means that we like different things, so we all have different qualities which make us special.'

Flora Kessell

Recently I have been talking to a young group of people who are lesbian, gay, bisexual and transgender. We have been discussing the challenges they face in their everyday lives. Many of the group experience disgusting remarks every day from the public, and many families can't accept them for who they are. The group also talked about the stereotypes of their sexualities. The members of the group are called Mohamed, Miles, Lisa and Rebeca. Mohamed and Rebeca have agreed for their stories to be told.

First I interviewed Rebeca. At the age of 18 Rebeca found her feet when she realised she didn't feel comfortable in her own body. She always thought she should have been born a boy. She found it hard to tell her family who she really was. She was 21 when she finally told them. She didn't get the reaction she was expecting.

Q: So what reaction did you get from your friends and family and how did you feel?

A: The reactions from my friends were mixed but it was the reaction of my family that really surprised me; they were amazing. Totally supportive, they accepted me for who I was. It was hard for the public to understand my decision though. Sometimes I didn't want to go outside because people would comment on what I was wearing or say, 'Make your mind up!' or 'What are you?' as if I was some sort of alien, but my amazing loyal friends and family helped me through.

Next I talked to Mohamed. He first realised that he was gay at the age of 15. He found it hard to tell his parents because he was Muslim. It was a faith that did not accept being gay. Mohamed was a very quiet boy and found it challenging when he had a big secret to hide. He came out on his 19th birthday. Mohamed was devastated by his family's reaction. His mother blamed herself and the family slowly fell apart. Mohamed's family disowned him. He was spat at in the street by men he knew from the mosque. Mohamed experienced some of the worst homophobia, particularly because he was a Muslim.

Q: Are you able to express your sexuality in public? Do people stereotype you for being gay?

A: I could never kiss my boyfriend in public. I couldn't even hold his hand. We would have to do it discreetly. If people realised they would say things like, 'Don't forget your purse!' or some women would assume that I was a fashion expert and say, 'You're gay aren't you? Would this go with my necklace?' People need to stop judging everyone and stereotyping gays, lesbians, bisexuals and transgender just because of someone else's view.

It really was amazing to hear what they have to experience every day and what challenges they have to overcome. They are no different from you or me. They respect us for our sexuality and so we should respect them for theirs.

Sophia Rivera Ramirez

Stereotype:

- **n. An over-simplified idea of the typical characteristics of a person or a thing.**
- **v. (stereotypes, stereotyping, stereotyped) view as a stereotype.**

Typical actions, typical behaviour and typical things *you* would say; in this case *they* would say. THEY are those who have no idea what an individual is going through, yet they label them, simply categorizing them due to their physical appearance or their intellect. The question is WHY? Why do *they* create false assumptions just to push the unique ones down? What do they have against US? They rip away our hope, our sanity, our escape from the pain, just for their pure amusement, forcing us to act exactly like in a coliseum. The freedom of being ourselves and being different is slipping through our fingertips whilst their vile words suffocate us. The fingers of the rumours lock around our throats trying desperately to cut off the air-supply. Because of this we hide behind the walls we have built in our minds to keep in who we want to be. We can't show the world who we really are. No, that's a sin. So we create the most plausible and realistic mask to cover us. Why? Because we are afraid, we are afraid of how we might be treated after they uncover the truth.

But that doesn't stop *them;* they gradually start the whispers again, which obviously makes *us* feel so small, so useless. That's when the negative thoughts enter our minds. Those thoughts begin to grow and grow and grow into small people called insecurities. Now the job of the insecurities is to take *their* side, to completely demolish the only confidence we have left. When the job is done we feel worthless. We start to think very dark thoughts that if *they* knew about the thoughts, *they* would be frightened to know that *they* cause them. The thoughts lead to us harming ourselves. You might think I am over-exaggerating a little, but trust me when I tell you that the only three words going through our minds are 'WASTE OF SPACE'. Why? They humiliate us by pointing out the most obvious flaws in each and every one of us, due to them planting subliminal messages in our subconscious.

Now the lack of trust is increasing dramatically which causes a lot of *us* to isolate ourselves from one another. That's their plan, to pull us apart so they can target us individually at our weakest points in life. They label us instead of using our personal names because to them we are nothing. We are too different, so we somehow became inferior and tumble all the way down to the bottom of the Status Hierarchy. The million dollar question is why do *they* go out of their way to make *us* feel like this? Well, you should feel lucky that I took the time to take all the possibilities into consideration...

They are afraid of who *we* truly are so they hide the status quo. It's ironic really how they ruin our self-esteem all because their self-esteem is probably lower.

But that doesn't stop *us* from fighting for what is right, from trying to be truly happy.

Berry Coleman

Ranga

Lots of people ask me, 'What is it like to be ginger?'

I never know whether to be offended or whether they are asking a genuine, sincere question. But if you ask me, I think it's fairly brave of them, considering we're known for our 'fiery tempers'! I thought that having ginger hair was just a genetic fact like having brown eyes, being short or having thick eyebrows. But from the dreaded Western World's point of view, having ginger hair means so much more.

Obviously, having ginger hair isn't exactly as common as brown, black or blonde – actually only 19% of the population are ginger. But why does such a minor thing that is actually quite common lead to those nasty stereotypes?

Is it because there's a kind of glamour to being different? Because we intimidate others? Because we're too individual? Who knows. But always remember that gingers don't know because they have no souls! And I'm pretty sure that if you have no soul then you don't know much. A brown-haired historian said that the basis of these stereotypes may lie in history. Even back in Ancient Egypt redheads were seen as witches and evil.

It isn't just the scientifically incorrect comments though. It's the constant drawing of attention to the fact that your hair has some orange undertones to it.

'Is that your natural hair colour?'

'Do you mind being ginger?'

'Woah, dude! I could totally see you from the other side of the field with that hair!'

You're not going to stop a brunette in the street and ask if that's their natural colour. And of course, you can't forget the 'Is it true that...' questions. It's fascinating, and really quite entertaining, to hear the tales of gingers. Apparently I'm not allowed out in the sun, otherwise I'll burn to a crisp, and who knew that my fellow gingers and me were related to Satan? Brilliant.

You cannot get away from it. A whole day was created in

celebration of redheads – 12th January, International Kiss a Ginger Day. And then of course, there's the Kick a Ginger Day – oh. And then there are the names that we go by, which you get used to: Carrot-top, Ginge, Ginga, Ginger Minger, Gingy, Firehead, Rusty, Ranga. At least we give away cheap jokes. We try and do things right, but when we do things wrong it's probably due to the fact that we're ginger, that's the explanation for most things. You can't get anything right. If you're naturally ginger you're inhuman, but if you dare dye your hair you're a traitor and then accused of being ashamed of being ginger.

Does it get better as you get older? The answer is no, not really. The stereotypes won't stop until you have nothing but white hair left. But the answer is to learn to tolerate it: don't give them a reaction and prove us the hot-headed people that we apparently are. Yes, I am ginger. Get over it.

Edith Wright

Poems

The Hide Aways

They're the hide aways,
The run away and shy aways,
The suicidal thoughts,
The magic road taunts,
The lesbian and gay beaten,
The self-harming weakened,
The hurt bullying victims,
With the thoughts of why them.
The cold and alone tonight,
Rest easy, don't let them put out your light…

STOP

Stop, he said
Stop, she said
But who cares about them?
It's their fault,
They're the nuts and bolts.
They're the bully victims,
Look away, glad it's not me,
Don't be a bystander!
STOP BULLYING NOW!
Don't just stand there, think how
You can help US, help THEM
Just stop, think…

Help Us

They hurt us,
They kick us,

More Than!

They punch us,
They stand there and laugh at us,
Just because we're different.
Don't stand and watch us,
Say something!
Stand out from the crowd!
We think, why me?
Just because we're different,
Just because we're different,
Just because we're different,
Help us...
Help me...

LGBT

Gay
Lesbian
Bisexual
Or Transgender
Stop right there!
Is it really that bad?
What's the point in sharing hate?
Do we really have to have a big debate?
They're not doing anything wrong,
So in conclusion of this stupid disapproval...

The Lovers

They're just in love, not breaking any laws.
There's nothing wrong with it,
Why are you making a fuss?
There's no need to cuss,
No need to barge into their lives,
No need to be rude,
No need to intrude,
Why would you care?
Return to your evil lair,
Just embrace it,

More Than!

Just accept it,
And don't hate!

Why

Why would you do that?
How could you do that?
It's inhumane,
Can't you see their pain?
Why are you bullying them?
It won't make anyone any happier,
How could you?
Why would you?
STOP
You laugh at them while they cry,
All I ask is why?

Don't worry
Don't worry,
Things are going to get easier,
Don't worry
The world will get much brighter,
Don't worry,
Keep it together,
Everything will be alright,
We'll set it right again,
And we can start again,
There will always be people that love you,
Never forget that,
Never lose that thought.

Just the way you are
You're not alone,
You'll never be alone,
You're perfect the way you are,
Like the song:
'Just the way you are'
If they call you names,
They're just playing games,

More Than!

They don't know,
They will never understand,
You know you're beautiful inside and out,
'Just the way you are' – perfect

Be Yourself

You are important and unique,
Don't listen to them,
You are amazing inside out and back again,
Don't let them change you,
Don't feel blue,
Don't let them pursue you.
Be yourself.
No matter who you love,
You should be free of
Fear, guilt and worry,
You should be free,
No matter what.

US

You can call us names,
You can abuse us,
You can put us down,
You can push us,
You can bully us,
You can force us,
Labels are for clothes, not people
Life gets better together
So…
You can love us,
You can hate us,
But you can't change us.

Sam Simmons

It was a regular night for Mr Smith. He slowly put on his dress and applied his makeup. He walked to the door and put on his high heels. He stumbled a bit and then stood up straight. He walked out of the door and walked down the street.

A group of kids were stood at the corner of his road. When they saw him walking past them they turned around and laughed quietly. He heard them snigger as he walked past and heard the words 'faggot' and 'bender' being tossed around. He walked as fast as he could in his heels to avoid hearing another hurtful word. He turned the corner and went straight into his local bar. He was greeted with icy stares and complete silence. The bartender stood up and looked him dead in the eye.

'What have I told you? We don't serve queers.'

'I have just as much right to be served as anyone here,' he replied, trembling with fear as he felt the eyes of everyone in the bar pointed towards him.

'Not in here you don't! Now leave before I make you leave!' the bartender spat at him.

He walked out sheepishly. The bartender's gaze followed him out.

He walked along the high street looking for a place to go. Families crossed the road to avoid him and teenagers walked into him. He got the dirtiest looks from everyone he walked past, and no-one stuck up for him when a group of people started hurling abuse towards him. He noticed a young girl running away from her parents in his direction. He picked her up to return her to her parents. She was snatched from his hands.

'Get your hands off my daughter!' her mother shouted in his face.

He kept walking down the street. He was holding back tears.

'When will I be accepted for who I am?' he thought to himself.

Slowly he walked home. He walked through a back-alley to avoid the abuse and cold stares he received as he walked through the street.

More Than!

'Why should I have to hide who I am?' he said to himself. 'Why can't people see who I really am?'

He got to his house and opened the door. All the lights were off and the house was silent. He walked up to the second floor and turned into the first room. His daughter was fast asleep. He leaned down and kissed her on the cheek. He went into his room. His wife was watching TV.

'Hi!' she said.

As he got into bed and started to fall asleep, he heard his wife say, 'I love you.'

Martha Jack

Please don't judge a book by its cover. I think we do far too much judging each other based on difference. It saddens me that we put people into certain stereotypical groups because of what they look like on the outside. In the end, we are all the same when we die. We are all skeletons on the inside.

In my opinion, stereotypes are used to keep everything in order. As humans we seek to group things together even if this means being shallow and judgmental. Some of the stereotypes floating around can put people off doing things with their lives.

For example, if your dream is to be a female weightlifter and someone tells you that this job is for boys because they are stronger, you might not want to follow this dream. Another example is that if a man was a drag queen, people would call him gay when in fact he leads a life with his wife and children. This might put him off doing what he loves.

This means that now there are a lot of people who want to be 'normal' and dress 'normally'. My question is, what is normal? Because if it means being average and like everyone else, then normal doesn't sound like fun. It sounds like hiding your personality for the benefit of others

Last year Disney made a movie called *The Lone Ranger*. In this movie the baddie has a cleft lip and palate. The actor who plays the baddie, William Fichtner, admitted that a prosthetic cleft was added with make-up to complete the 'look' of a villain and that 'having a broken nose and cleft lip made it easier to slip into the role of the villain'. The film studio decided to give him a 'terribly scarred face', which is apparently 'a perfect reflection of the bottomless pit that passes for his soul'. I find what Disney did extremely offensive and untrue to say the least because I have a cleft lip and palate. It makes me feel that when I'm walking down the street, people who have watched this movie will associate me with this horrible villain. In Victorian times people with a facial difference were considered freaks and possibly created by witchcraft. I am disappointed that, in the modern world, Disney thinks it's okay to use facial difference to indicate badness.

More Than!

It seems a shame to place labels on people. Since, if we are lucky, we will live to be eighty, in our lives we should have the chance to explore ourselves, all of our selves, and not be trapped under a label of other people's making. I believe that we should be able to be who we are. I think the worst thing about labels is that they might limit who we think we are and can be.

Imagine a world where everyone looked the same. Difference is what makes the world interesting. If humans were all the same, imagine how bland and boring that would be. How we look is a big part of our personality and the culture that we are part of. We should feel proud to be who we are.

Marilyn Ferizaj

> **Before you speak....**
> **T.H.I.N.K.**
> **T – Is it True?**
> **H – Is it Helpful?**
> **I – Is it Inspiring?**
> **N – Is it Necessary?**
> **K – Is it Kind?**

If you really know how it affects a person when they have been judged or taken advantage of, then you will know how much it hurts. Words or judgements can build us up, break us down, start a fire in our hearts and put it out. Even though the tongue has no bones, that doesn't mean it can't break our hearts.

The 'gay boy' you punched in the hall today
Committed suicide a few minutes ago.
That girl you called a 'slut' in class today,
She's a virgin.
That boy you called 'lame',
He has to work every night to support his family.
That girl you pushed down the other day,
She's already being abused at home.
That girl you called 'fat',
She's starving herself.
The old man you made fun of because of his 'ugly scars',
He fought for our country.
The boy you made fun of for crying,
His mother is dying.
The teacher you called a 'druggie'
Is dying of cancer.

More Than!

No matter what you think or see, there's always something more to a person. Always something you don't know about them. Everyone has their own secrets and insecurities. It's sad that others are just so careless and don't consider how other people feel. It's sad how someone has to emotionally collapse for people to notice them. Don't judge – you never know when you might just find yourself in that person's shoes. It's funny how the people who know least about you have the most to say about you.

Stereotypes lose their power when the world is found to be more complex than the stereotype would suggest. When we learn that individuals do not fit the group stereotype, then it begins to fall apart. No-one, including yourself, would ever like to be judged in a negative way. Even though stereotypes do exist, we can avoid them by walking through them. The whole idea of a stereotype is to simplify instead of going through the problem of all this great diversity – that it's this or maybe that – you have just one statement. It is this:

Nobody is perfect and nobody deserves to be perfect. Nobody has it easy, everybody has issues. You never know what people are going through. So pause before you start judging, criticizing or mocking others. Everybody is fighting their own unique war.

Think twice before you speak, because your words and influence will plant the seed of either success or failure in the mind of another.

Watch your thoughts,
They become words.

Watch your words,
They become actions.

Watch your actions,
They become habits.

Watch your habits,
They become your character.

More Than!

Watch your character,
It becomes your destiny.

Lorna Beckett

I'm a child so I must be naïve, be innocent.
In fact, I've lived through a war and am now doing my GCSEs early.

I'm a teenager so I must be a trouble-causer, have attitude, be moody.
In fact, I volunteer in a homeless shelter and always step aside for prams in the street.

I'm old so I must be a grandparent, be frail, be slow, be retired, be wise.
In fact, I'm a fulltime lawyer and swim every other day.

I'm gay so I must be flamboyant, love fashion, be feminine, be a drama queen.
In fact, I coach a professional rugby team and wear trainers and scruffy tracksuits.

I'm lesbian so I must be a tomboy, be unfeminine, be feisty, have short hair.
In fact, I work in a designer clothes shop and attend ballet classes every week.

I'm a feminist so I must hate men, be unattractive, be whiny, be single.
In fact, I'm married with two children and work as a model.

I'm a Muslim so I must be a terrorist, be sexist, be conservative.
In fact, I am a doctor who is fighting against female genital mutilation.

I'm disabled so I must be stupid, be crippled, be unable to communicate.
In fact, all my grades are well above average and I go to wheelchair basketball training every Monday.

More Than!

I'm obese so I must eat too much on purpose, have no self-control.
In fact, I have a rare disorder that causes my fat levels to increase without a trigger.

I'm black so I must be in a gang, be from Africa, be dangerous, be on drugs.
In fact, I'm a chemistry student from Holland and have never taken drugs in my life.

I'm English so I must be white, be rich, be posh, live in London, love the royals.
In fact, I'm mixed race, live on a council estate in Hull and hate the queen.

I'm a boy so I'm not in touch with my feelings, never cry.

I'm a girl so I don't like maths, science or any sports.

Every human is a different equation, a different concoction of specialised ingredients.

Every human deserves to be their own person – stereotypes limit us to the label we've been given, to the characteristics that society has chosen for us.

But we know that we're more than that, we know that we should fight for who we are as individuals.

We know that we should, no matter what anyone says, be OURSELVES.

Shay Snipe Gayle

For the purpose of this assignment I interviewed my Uncle Peter to see what it was like growing up in the '70s as a gay person. I asked him a various amount of questions about him growing up. I was with my mum and my Uncle Peter on his couch and then I started to ask him questions. I started with:

'Who did you first tell?'

'I first told my cousin Teressa when I was nineteen years old.'

'How did you feel when you told your cousin?'

'It was very difficult because she had asked me once before and I told her no, and straight after I said no I was kicking myself because I knew she was trying to help me. I also wasn't comfortable to talk about it.'

'What was it like growing up?'

'Growing up was really difficult because kids were calling me names and I had a lot of name-calling in my childhood because when you're a child and you're different, they will say something. But it's not something you choose, it's who you are. That made me not feel bad about myself.'

'When did you realise that you were gay?'

'I knew I was gay when I was sixteen or seventeen years old.'

'Were your family okay with you being gay?'

'I'm not sure because I've not really come out to my family as such. I had an uncle who was gay so I found it easy to speak to him, he supported me.'

'What difficulties did you encounter?'

'When people found out, straight away they would call me names that I didn't like, and people weren't going to accept me for who I was.'

'Did you have any role models when you were growing up?'

'There weren't that many role models in the '70s because most people stereotyped lots of people.'

'How did your close friends take it that you were gay?'

'It was a mixed reaction with my friends. I was scared of rejection from them, I thought they wouldn't speak to me anymore.'

'Have things changed for the better?'

'Certainly, now we are being recognised for who we are and that has to be a good thing.'

'Did you ever think of suicide?'

'No, but I knew someone who did. His name was Terry and this was when I was seventeen years old. He was mixed race and he came out to his family that he was gay and his family would beat him, physically beat him. Unfortunately, he couldn't take it so he jumped off a tower block and died.'

I was so very sad to hear what happened to my uncle's friend. I can't believe he passed away like that. I'm so glad I was born in this era. No matter what sexuality you are, you should be treated the same as everyone else. My uncle also works as a teacher, but to hear what he went through really inspires me to knock out whatever comes in my way and carry on my life.

Milly Mason

If I lay here amongst the trees I will be free
Because trees don't have the eyes to judge,
They don't have the mouths for abuse
The trees are harmless
So If I lay here forever I will be okay
And one day my body will slowly join the earth
My spirit will thrive
Amongst the clouds
Over our destruction
I won't be a label
My tag will untie
The string will be loosened
I will be free
To smile,
To laugh,
To breathe
To live.

When it goes quiet behind my eyes
I can leave my mind to wander
It can wander through empty streets
Where first impressions don't exist

I am more than my body.
My arms,
My legs,
My features,
My hair,
That is only half of my being.

So when I lay here,
Amongst the trees
I am no longer sick

More Than!

I do not have a sexuality
I'm not male
Nor am I female
I am my spirit
And I am my soul
I won't have a purpose
But that's fine with me,
I am as relevant as the ground I step on,
I am as free as the running water
I am as wild as the sea.

So I lay down at night
I look up at the stars
And they look at me
A symbolisation of my many worries
Set free.

We become so numb to what we speak
But I guess people are people
And they all have something to say
But here,
In my world,
The trees mutter kindness
And the breeze whispers humour.

I am not alone
I am among many companions
They don't hurt me
They cannot hurt me
They won't hurt me
They listen
They always listen
I can speak to them for hours
They understand
And sometimes
If I really listen to them
I can hear them whisper back to me.

Cassius Burley

Lack of equality: one of the world's biggest problems. Lack of equality exists in many areas including race, gender and LGBT (lesbian, gay, bisexual and transgender). Equality is the concept that all people should be treated equally and be given equal rights no matter where they come from or who they are. It is absurd that anyone would think someone is less of a person because of the colour of their skin, or their sex, or their gender. Or is it?

I wanted to interview some people I know about equality. People who say they believe in equality, but I will find out if they really do.

My father is Leo Burley; he is 50 years old and he is a white British middle-class man.

Q: Do you think everyone is equal?

A: No, but I think they should be, especially in terms of education and access to it.

Q: Did you go to a state school or a public school?

A: I went to a public school between the ages of 11 to 14.

Q: Have you ever been racist?

A: Yes.

Q: In what way?

A: When I was growing up I used a racist word in jokes because I thought they were funny, but later I learnt that they were offensive to people of colour. I also sang anti-Semitic songs at football matches as a joke until I learnt that many Jewish people found this very offensive.

More Than!

Q: Do you know any LGBT people?

A: Yes, I know many.

Q: Have you ever discriminated against LGBT people?

A: Yes. I've used homophobic language, often in jokes, without thinking carefully about the words I was using. I try not to use language like that today.

Q: Do you think LGBT people are equal to all others?

A: I think they should be treated equally.

Q: If you think LGBT people should be treated equally then why have you used homophobic language?

A: I do not have a very good answer to that question. It may be due to the fact that I was not educated about LGBT issues and prejudice when I was at school.

My brother is called Cyrus Burley; he is 6 years old and a white British boy.

Q: Do you know what equality is?

A: No.

Q: What do you think it is?

A: I think it is when people are equal.

Q: Do you think everyone should be equal?

A: Yes.

Q: Why?

A: Because then it will be fair.

More Than!

Q: Do you think everyone is equal and if so, why?

A: No, I think that some people are not equal in other people's views – like men and women, because men think women aren't as good at things as men are.

Q: Do you think lack of equality is a problem?

A: Yes, I want all people to have the same rights.

Me, Cassius Burley, aged 12 and a white British male.

Q: Is everyone equal?

A: I quote George Orwell: 'All animals are equal, but some animals are more equal than others.'

Rachel Finke

Birds twitter in the distance, chirping merrily to one another. The wind blows softly, as sudden gusts cause the autumn leaves to dance and swirl around my feet. For an autumn in London it is a pleasant day, accentuated by the shining sun. Lighthearted, with a slight skip in my step, I continue to stroll down the quiet street. I pass a newsagent and a newspaper headline in the window catches my eye: *London Terror Warning – Attacks Likely.*

Although this ought to concern me, I decide that there are happier things to think about. I have been making similar decisions more and more often recently, choosing not to ponder over miserable things. Happy is good, happy is safe.

Happiness.

Happiness, undoubtedly one of life's most important aspects, is starting to come to me much more easily these days. I look back at the past few years and shudder at the thought of them. They seem so... gloomy. It's as if a thick, grey mist has manipulated its way into my memories, suffocating the joy from every nook and cranny. Not that there was much joy in the first place. This stretch of road is my healing process, and its end is in my sight. Everything seems so simple, so happy right now. If I could freeze time, I would freeze it here.

As I reach the bus-stop, I glance up to check the time for the next bus. Due. The shambling bus rolls up and I get on. Everything is perfect.

Perfect.

I want it to stay this way. Stay this way so that I can keep the smile on my face and the joy in my heart. Compared with the empty street the bus is surprisingly full and I can't find an available seat. Instead I stand, waiting for one. As a woman gets up and off the bus, she leaves an empty seat behind her and I glance around. Someone might need the seat more than me. As far as I can tell nobody does and I take the seat, relaxing as I sit down. The man next to me smells of sweat. This probably isn't his fault, as for the time of year the day is considerably warm. He's reading the paper which had the terrorism headline and keeps giving me sideways glances. This makes me feel uncomfortable and I stare back at him.

'What are you looking at?' he hisses. 'Stupid Muslims. You're a terrorist, that's what you are. You all are! Well, we don't want you!'

This is all said rather loudly and suddenly everybody on the bus is staring. Some glare at the man as he gets up and leaves, but others glare at *me*. I feel my eyes prickle with tears. *Don't show you're weak. Don't cry.*

Don't.

Don't let it get to you. Everything has gone quiet, but nothing is said. I've been left angry, hurt and shocked. That's all it took, one word, 'Terrorist', and what looked to be a happy day is ruined.

Tamar Singer

The Lawyer

Ugh, it's so annoying having to go to work on a Saturday! Tim gets to stay at home because he's freelance but you can't be a stupid lawyer and work from home. At least if I get these last two cases cleared up now, I won't have to work on them during our honeymoon. Can you imagine that?

Mum's quite shocked that we're finally getting round to this marriage since we never got a civil partnership thingy, but now they've passed this new law letting us it felt ungrateful not to.

I squidge up to the wall and let this girl in a wheelchair pass, then some batty old lady. Here's me complaining and really I should be glad I'm not like that! I pull out my glasses and let my book fall open. My app says the bus will be thirteen minutes so I might as well. Suddenly a little girl runs up to me and grabs my book. A woman – probably her childminder: a different colour to the kid – yells at the girl, who jumps, hands me back my book, mutters and scampers away.

The Teenager

```
im gonna be 18 soz
        how lng?
dunno ☹
        no point coming if 18r than 4
OK TTYL
        whr r u now?
busstop
        ☺
im sittin NXT 2 DIS total weirdo.. bet shez
lesbian
        i knO wot U mean
& crip shez gonna mAk it tAk lng!
        k TLK 2 U 18r
```

More Than!

```
        dad mAd me come hOm ☹ soz
cant cum til 5
        y
pickin up sis
        y cnt ur mum?
Shez sic again. i hav 2 do evrytng
        still sic?
NEway shutup bout mum
        soz didn't think
c U soon @ chippy
        c u soon
```

The Old Lady

Dear Helena,

We haven't spoken for ages so I thought I'd better write.

Today was a typical day. I visited Daniel at the hospital and went shopping. They finally told us Daniel's cancer was incurable, but to be honest I already knew that.

At the bus stop I got a real scare! I know it seems silly and youngsters aren't what we think but there was this black boy on his phone and a hood covering his face. He was about 16 and pulled out something that I thought was a gun! Turned out it wasn't but I got so frightened.

There was also a really grumpy woman whose kids kept asking for their dad. They obviously loved her husband more than her.

Hope to speak soon,
Linda

The Disabled Woman

Dear Diary,

I must be such a nuisance! This chair is so bulky! When I squeezed past this businessman today, he gave me a really sympathetic look. I bet he's got a nice wife to do all the work though. He was working on Saturday though. Also there was this lesbian who was so grumpy! At least I think she was lesbian 'cause her kids were adopted (different skin colour) and she dressed like a lesbian. Don't most lesbians have short hair too?

Daniel-James Straughan

Behind Closed Doors

It's not just my generation who are living in a diverse world of many individuals seeking to find equality. For many centuries, in many cultures, in many countries round the world, being Lesbian, Gay, Bisexual or Transgender has been clouded with stigma and treated as a crime against religion and God's will for the continued existence of humankind.

History will tell you how people were put on trial and imprisoned merely for being a Lesbian, Gay or Bisexual, and most recently in these past few decades, Transgender. People have lost their lives as a punishment for going against their cultures and religion. This terrible and unjust treatment continues to happen in our current and diverse world today. Many innocent people have been attacked, leaving them severely injured, and on some occasions people have been killed. Many, sadly, have taken their own lives by committing suicide.

It seems that the general consensus is based on us being born with pre-programmed sexual preferences. Male to female. Girlfriends with boyfriends. Husbands with wives. Pink for girls. Blue for boys. No room for in between or being different.

I have not experienced on a personal level the emotional pain and deep hurt that others have had to face. I have family members who are Lesbian and Gay. I have known family friends who are Lesbian and Gay. They are not freaks or monsters. They do not make me feel scared or freaked out. They are my family, they are my friends. I do not talk to them differently because of their sexual preferences. I do not love them less or differently because of their sexual preferences. There is good and bad in every person. No matter what their sexual preference is.

I decided to put together some questions and use them to interview friends and family who are both Gay and Lesbian.

I wanted to see inside the world where innocent people are shunned, their loves kept secret, and share the hidden pain experienced by so many.

The persons I have interviewed are a mixture of family and friends, some who are known to me, and some who I have never met before.

These are just some of their experiences.

This is Sue's story.

When did you first realise you were a Lesbian?

I knew I was different as early as age 7, but never really knew or understood it and acted on it when I was 14. I knew from age 14 I was a Lesbian.

How difficult was it to share with your family, friends and/or work colleagues such personal details?

I found it very difficult. My family were very old-fashioned, and I was raised to believe that life for a woman was about getting married and raising children. My grandmother raised me, and although I found it hard to tell her, when I did she was amazing and embraced my partners as part of the family.

I lost other family members because they didn't accept me, and they still remain very distant in my life, or are not in it at all. I have learnt to live with the fact and it no longer hurts because I only have people in my life who accept me for who I am.

My friends all guessed, so that part was difficult at school, but those closest to me understood and accepted me for who I was. I am visually an obvious lesbian, so I don't have the need to come out to work colleagues or anyone else, so I openly talk about my girlfriend and my life without hiding or explaining.

What challenges have you faced? Were these family or work-related? Do you still face these now?

The first real challenge I had, and the first time I experienced homophobia I was 17. A male work colleague hit on me and I wanted to be honest with him so I told him that I was gay. He was shocked and told me I was disgusting. He and three other males waited for me one night when I left work. They dragged me to a nearby towpath by the canal and beat me up. They also tried to rape me. A man out walking saw this happening and chased them off. I never went to the police – we didn't have the laws to protect us that we have now, and I was too scared to admit that I was gay. I never returned to my job and I became a hermit for almost six months. This had a very damaging psychological effect on me. I felt hated by the world and abnormal, but I just couldn't live a lie or present myself in the world looking and dressing the way almost all other women did. I had the support of my grandmother and a couple of other family members, and they helped me to be strong again. I went to the gym every day and vowed that no-one would ever hurt me again. I became strong both emotionally and physically.

I have had other instances of men wanting to hurt me because of the way that I look, but only one other occasion when it got physical. Up until my late thirties I always got verbal abuse from strangers but never from anyone that knew me. I am now 45, and as I age I get less verbal abuse. I still get stared at and evil looks but nothing compared to my younger days. I still think that we have a long way to go before people accept the LGBT community and stop homophobia.

Do you feel more free and liberated and able to be yourself now that people know about your sexuality? Or do you sometimes feel that you still have to hide your true self?

I feel safer than I did twenty years ago now that laws are in place and people are more accepting, so I do feel that I can walk down the street without so much fear, but I will feel liberated when I can walk down the street holding my girlfriend's hand without fear. I get abuse and threats when I do this. What most people take for granted I can't do, and sometimes it is just sharing the moment and wanting to hug or kiss your partner in public. I have to think about these things and not do them for risk of harm to me or my partner. I am openly gay to everyone in my life. I don't care what people think any more, and those that matter don't care what gender my partner is. I am proud of who I am and I no longer hide. I'm not sure that I would call it liberated; I'd say that I'm sick of hiding and now strong enough to be who I am, and visible to the world.

What advice would you give to someone who wants to 'come out' about their sexuality?

My advice is to be who you are and be proud of the person that you are. Don't let people put you down for your sexuality/gender. Always fight for your place in the world. No-one has a right to put you down for the choices that you make for your own happiness. Don't change to make others happy. Pressure from others to be different than you really are can make you make the wrong choices and you will end up paying for it later or hurting others. Always be aware of danger, and those that don't have an open mind. Things might have moved on but there are still those narrow-minded people in the world that don't accept you.

Timing is key to coming out. Don't think that you need to tell the world all in one day. You will know when the time is right, or you might not, but don't rush. Sometimes people close to us don't want to hear it. But they already know it, so it can be left unspoken.

When I came out I never had the internet. I wish that I did. Use it, research, get support, it is all out there. Don't feel alone because you are not, and never feel that what you feel or experience is wrong. We don't choose who we love, we just go with the heart and what feels right for us, no matter how different that might be to most of the people around you, it works for you and that is what matters. We have one life, live it for you.

This is Laura's story:

When did you first realise you were Lesbian, Gay, Bisexual or Transgender?

Originally I was twelve years old when I had my first girlfriend. My mum found out about 18 months later and I was forbidden to see her again. Finally we are back together 27 years later. In between I had boyfriend after boyfriend.

How difficult was it to share with your family, friends and/or work colleagues such personal details?

No-one knew about my first love except my mum – who went ballistic. I was too young, it wasn't normal... blah blah. This time round, all family and friends have been fab... even my mum.

Do you feel more free and liberated and able to be yourself now that people know about your sexuality? Or do you sometimes feel you still have to hide your true self?

Definitely. Although I kind of feel like 'I am me, take me or leave me'... not changing for anyone.

What advice would you give to someone who wants to 'come out' about their sexuality?

Do it as soon as possible and be brave, and think... you loved me before you knew... what's changed? If you don't like the answer, then they weren't worth it anyway.

This is Luddle's story:

When did you first realise you were a Lesbian, Gay, Bisexual or Transgender?

At a very young age, possibly 9 or 10. I had an erotic dream about He-Man when I was very young! I came out when I was 25/26 – what a waste, eh?

How difficult was it to share with your family, friends and/or work colleagues such personal details?

Not hard. I came out more because I couldn't be bothered to be in anymore. I could see it really wasn't an issue. I came out to pals first, then family, then work. I have always been quite confident, so quickly adopted the approach that I didn't really care what other people thought, as long as I was being true to myself, and not hurting anyone in the process.

What challenges have you faced? Were these family or work-related? Do you still face these now?

I went to an all-boys school, played rugby, and my dad's a roofer, but to be honest none of these things were an issue for me. The problem was just plucking up the courage to tell someone. Better education from an early age would have been hugely beneficial. No, I don't have any problems.

Do you feel more free and liberated and able to be yourself now that people know about your sexuality? Or do you sometimes feel that you still have to hide your true self?

Coming out is the best thing ever, which is why I say the sooner the better. Don't be penned in by staying in. For me, coming out gave me freedom, true confidence, and a new lease of life.

What advice would you give to someone who wants to 'come out' about their sexuality?

Just do it, sooner the better. Although anything sexual should be age-appropriate. Don't be too eager to label yourself. Don't be ashamed to explore, and be open about it.

This is Judy's family story:

The first I knew of homosexuality in my family was when my mum told me about her brother Alfie. He apparently told her when he was about seventeen – that would be about 1942. When he told her that he thought he was homosexual she asked him if he would get better. Such were the times. She didn't know what the word meant, let alone that it was illegal and carried a prison sentence if found out. He was by all accounts a gentle boy, artistic, with a love of classical music. He was the apple of his mother's eye and dearly loved by his sisters – my

More Than!

mum Elise and Josie and Irene. Granddad wasn't quite so enamoured of him, it seems, referring to him once or twice as 'a bit of a nancy boy'. Nan always defended him, I believe, but, well, times were what they were. Granddad died aged only 44 in 1944 so I would hope the pressure was off for a little while. Alfie joined the RAF in '43 (aged 18), but having read his service records, his time there was a bit of a mystery. He travelled around quite a bit, trained as a navigator, and went here, there and everywhere. Sadly his story came to an end in 1947. Aged just 22 he committed suicide while stationed in Zeltweg, Austria, and is buried in Klagenfurt. I visited his grave in 2013, having promised my mum I would shortly before she died. It was moving to say the least, but he was at least afforded a military grave in a beautiful setting in a war cemetery.

Here is where the story gets a little bizarre. I am pretty sure now that Mum's sister Irene was also gay, but I can never be sure. She suffered from manic depression (bipolar as we now know it) and also took her own life in 1973, aged 46. Perhaps this too was because she was afraid to come out. I will never know. So my dear Nan lost two children to suicide. ☹

Moving on... Although I was born and bred in East London, we moved to Somerset in 1974. My son and my mum were always particularly close, sometimes to excess. She was protective of him. Although he looks incredibly like his dad, he also bears a striking resemblance to Alfie. And here history starts to repeat... Adam was never into sport or anything remotely masculine. His interests always veered towards the artistic. We can see where this is going. His schooldays were dogged by bullying. He always had a trail of girls following him around, and I guess the boys were at first jealous, then plain violent. I spent days and days speaking to teachers etcetera, but have to say none were interested. Adam was born in 1973 and the nonsense started in about '85/6. Mum first mentioned it to me. It was never a problem, though: we just wanted him to be safe and happy. I was slightly surprised when a teacher called me in one day, suggested Adam may be gay, and that I should talk to our GP, for heaven's sake! Stupid woman.

Our town was never kind to Adam. Just like in school he was bullied, not only by the kids but some of the parents. His ambition since he was about four years old was to be a hair-

More Than!

dresser, nothing else would do. He pursued his dream but felt the need to get out of West Somerset at the earliest possible opportunity. He followed his heart, applied to all the top salons in London. He was offered several interviews and set off. Following on, he was then offered several jobs. The rest, as they say, is history. He is still living in London and is co-owner of two rather well-known salons. The past is now another land and he is comfortable with who he is, but I believe there are still scars. I know I have them, for whoever hurts my children, hurts me.

And so to the present day. My seventeen-year-old granddaughter is at the moment in a relationship with another girl. She admits that she still fancies boys, but at the moment is happy where she is. Has she ever been bullied about it? NO. Have times changed? Well, when her girlfriend came out to her mother, her response was, 'I would rather you had told me you had cancer.' So in some ways it has got easier; sadly, though, there is still so much prejudice.

It was never a problem to me or Adam's dad or sisters. As long as he and my granddaughter are safe then the world can 'do one'! Ha ha x

Attitudes are still mixed, but to my mind, as long as homosexuality is spoken about, discussed openly, and not ridiculed because it's not quite the norm, then progress is being made. And thanks to your son, well, the world is a better place xx

I hope this is of some use to Dan. I am full of admiration for his project, and if he has any questions then please ask. I will answer anything. ☺

Also available from Team Angelica Publishing

'Reasons to Live' by Rikki Beadle-Blair
'What I Learned Today' by Rikki Beadle-Blair

'Faggamuffin' by John R Gordon
'Colour Scheme' by John R Gordon
'Souljah' by John R Gordon

'Fairytales for Lost Children' by Diriye Osman

'Black & Gay in the UK – an anthology' edited by John R Gordon & Rikki Beadle-Blair

'Tiny Pieces of Skull' by Roz Kaveney

'Slap' by Alexis Gregory